THE
FLYING DUTCHMAN,
OR THE
DEMON SHIP.

CHAPTER I.

PERIOD—1640.

THE WIDOW AND HER SON—DESPAIR AND DEATH.

AMSTERDAM was, in the year 1640, a rapidly progressing town; the union of the states of Zeeland and Holland with Brabant and Flanders, in 1578, in the pacification of Ghent, was the mainspring to its rise in prosperity. The great advantages which it offered in a commercial point of view attracted tradesmen and merchants from the surrounding provinces, and indeed from all parts of Europe, in thousands; ships from all

NO. I.

parts of the world arrived, bearing the richest merchandise; and the town, which scarcely two hundred years preceding was a collection of a few huts, surrounded by a weak palisade to protect it from the incursions of the inhabitants of Utrecht, had, at the time we mention, spread into a fine city, possessing streets upwards of one hundred and forty feet wide, and containing houses the splendour of which would do honour to any town in Europe. It was in the outskirts of this city, in a street called Floris Graat, named after Count **Floris,** who, in 1275, exempted the town from paying certain taxes, and who was the first on record that named the place, which occurs in a letter of his, wherein he exempts Amstelre-damme, a spot containing a few fishermen's huts, from the dues to which they were liable—it was in this street there stood a small, neat house, one which, ten years preceding, was in all its pride of youth and beauty, but now, from neglect, its external beauty was rapidly on the decline. Like most of the houses in Amsterdam, it was built of brick, and had been painted and neatly decorated with tiles of various colours, but white, blue, and green were predominant; there was a little garden belonging to it, but the flowers were faded and choked with weeds; altogether there was a desolate look about the house — one might judge there was sorrow and misery attached to it. We may often read the story of the inhabitants of a house from its exterior, as you may a man's character from his personal appearance; grief stamps, with an iron impress, whatever it clasps in its withering embrace. In a room on the ground floor, on a high-backed chair surrounded by pillows, sat a female, whose faded black dress, weeds and coif, proclaimed her a widow; she appeared old, yet upon a close inspection it was but the effects of some terrible grief preying upon her mind, which produced the appearance of premature old age; she had not numbered two short years beyond forty, yet her wrinkled face, her drawn mouth, and lined forehead, added ten years to her look; her eyes were brilliant to an extreme — it is ever the character of disease and misery; her voice was weak and faint, and her breath so short that she drew it to every sentence she uttered; it was evident that she was the victim of a mental calamity,—some awful stroke of destiny which comes upon our feelings like the lightning's shaft upon the green tree, it blasts its fresh-ness for ever, leaving it a withered and blackened memento of its terrible power: opposite to her, upon a chair, seated in a careless, easy manner, was a young man about one-and-twenty; he was strongly and well-formed; his limbs were firmly knit, and betokened, did occasion require it, the possession of great strength; his long fair hair fell smooth from his forehead until it reached his neck, where it terminated in short, thick curls; he had full blue eyes, which flashed with a reckless daring of expression, and betrayed his character instantly to the beholder; his nose was straight and well-defined, while his lips had the appearance of thick-ness, from a constant curl of scorn and impatience; he seemed to rest uneasily in his chair, for he kept changing his position, throwing himself from one side to the other, but always keeping the attitude of great care-lessness; his brow bore a cloud, and, from the gloom which shadowed his countenance, it might be judged the conversation that was passing was not much to his satisfaction.

"Mother," he exclaimed, " long illness has made you weak-minded, you are frightened at shadows; let me have my wish; my life is as likely to be taken from me in any occupation as it is in that of a sailor: have we not ships which leave this port for years together, each voyage, with nearly the same crew? Look at my uncle, your own brother, has he not been on the sea these five-and-twenty years, and did he not come home a short time since as well as ever he was? Is he not gone again with his vessel manned by the same crew that have worked the ship these last four voyages; and have not many of the men been with him since he first trod the ship as commander?"

"It may be so, Albert," replied the widow, "but I have an unconquerable dread of the sea—a horror which nothing can mitigate—the name alone almost excites me to frenzy; as you love me, I implore you, my dear boy, do not trust its treacherous bosom, for if you once quit me for that purpose, we shall never, never meet again; I know it, I feel it here," and she pressed her hand to her breast.

"Why, mother, what do you fear?" asked Albert. "Think you, because my poor father met with a watery grave, I must needs share the same fate?"

"Do not question me," replied his mother, "do not, I implore you, mention that circumstance to me; it revives recollections of maddening agony. Albert, Albert, you must not leave me for the sea!"

"What am I to do?" retorted her son. "I have no knowledge of any handicraft that I can pursue; I have health, strength—I am at the age of manhood—we are miserably poor; and am I to stop here in wretchedness, and see you pine away in want and misery, and forego the only chance I have of placing you in comfort? Your brother has offered me an excellent situation in his vessel; and, with a stout heart and a good will, I shall live to make your declining days a blessing to yourself and to me, dear mother."

"Never, never," earnestly uttered the Widow Vanderdecken; "it cannot be, it cannot be."

"Why not?" impatiently asked Albert, and he drew himself up proudly as he continued: "Mother, am I unworthy to be trusted? I have been wayward and wilful, but never mean or dishonourable; I am the only, at least I am the nearest, and, I hope, the dearest tie you have; why am I kept ignorant of a secret which I know is of great importance, and concerns me, indirectly it may be, but it concerns me as I am connected with you; tell me, mother, if you have faith in me—and I have never yet wronged your trust in me; is the reason of your abhorrence to the sea connected with the room which has been closed ever since my childhood, too long for me to remember aught respecting it?"

In the earnestness of his appeal Albert had fixed his eyes upon his mother, and saw with alarm that she was labouring under violent agitation; it increased so powerfully that she pressed her hands convulsively upon her neck and breast, which was heaving with frightful rapidity, and seemed striving with terrible exertion to keep herself from choking. Albert flew to her side, and exclaimed—

"Mother, mother, for God's sake tell me why is this violent emotion? lean your head on my breast,—there, you are better; for Heaven's sake what does this all mean? Whenever I have mentioned that room, your agitation has been terrible; tell me, I conjure you."

"I will, Albert," at length faintly articulated the widow, as she slightly recovered the excitement which the mention of the room had produced; "I will tell you, for I feel the hand of death is upon me, and this may be the only chance which nature may leave me, and it is fit you know the dreadful circumstances which caused the closing of that chamber. Heaven grant me strength to go through with the horrid tale; oh, Almighty Power! thou knowest the bitter anguish which has been mine since the horrors of that night: may what I have suffered avert calamity from my child, and alleviate HIS awful punishment! Albert, Albert, when I have told you, when you learn—I—I—bear with me, my child, my heart will break," and, sobbing with violence, she buried her head on his breast.

"Mother, dear mother, your illness and our sad circumstances have preyed upon your mind and depressed your spirits to an extreme," soothingly exclaimed Albert. "We have all our share of grief in life, you have had much, very much, but the time will come when you will live happily and smile joyously on me, when you have those comforts round you which it will be my pride and glory to obtain for you."

"No, Albert," cried the widow, with a startling clearness of voice which surprised him, "no, Albert, it is a kind thought, but a vain hope; my hours are numbered, I am dying."

"Say not so, mother," interrupted Albert.

"Do not interrupt me, my child, but listen while I have the strength left me, which I feel is granted to me for the purpose of disclosing to you the secret which has been the worm that has eaten my brain, gnawing ceaselessly from that time until now, blasting every thing, making every thought an agony. Albert, your father was a bold, daring, high-spirited man, one who laughed at dangers as shadows to frighten children and fools with; you possess much of his temper, too much of his spirit and recklessness; may you never be punished for its wildness—not as he has been, I pray God, I pray God! He left me, Albert, eighteen years ago, full of spirits and happiness, in all the richness of manly health and pride of manly beauty, the captain of a noble ship named after this city, the Amstelredamme, on a voyage to the Indies; in all his voyages he had been prosperous, very prosperous, and he had promised me that it should be the last, if it proved as successful as his former ones: I had extorted this promise from him, for I could not feel happy while he was away from me for months, months—aye, twelve and fourteen long months have I been separated at one time from him. You were born then; a young child scarce three years old, I could not bear to be parted from him, and labouring under the horrid idea that each day might bring me the news of the loss of his ship and of his death; I urged him with all the persuasion I possessed, and he consented to live a life of indolence, which was foreign to his nature, to make me happy, for he loved me deeply and devotedly, as I loved him—and beyond *that* love nothing could pass. He had been away from me eight long months, years they seemed, for I dwelt with fondness on his return never more to leave me; we had had unusually stormy weather for more than a week, I had noted it with fearful attention; in the long nights, when the wind howled and shook the window-frames. I laid and listened with fear and trembling to every fitful gust, and prayed that he might not become a victim to the wrath of the wind and waves—

that he might be restored to me in safety. One night, after violent rain in the day, it set in a fearful gale; the wind roared with a fury which I have never since witnessed; trees were torn up by the roots, houses were unroofed, and the house rocked on its foundation. I laid you down in your cradle, and sung you to sleep with a song which your father loved to hear me sing to him—the words were written by his mother in the absence of her husband, who was a sailor; your father taught me the words, but since that night they have never passed my lips. I will repeat them to you; should you ever again hear them, you will know that the utterer is connected with you by some strange and near tie; they ran thus :—

Thou art not here, beloved one,
    To cheer me with thy smile,
I cannot know, beloved one,
    One single joy, the while
            Thou art not here,
                    Dear love.

The flowers and skies, beloved one,
    Are sweet and bright to-day;
Yet all things seem, beloved one,
    In gloom when thou'rt away.
            Thou art not here,
                    Dear love.

The sweetest birds, beloved one,
    Breathe songs of silv'ry tone;
Yet, ah! to me, beloved one,
    No voice is like thine own.
            Thou art not here,
                    Dear love.

Return to me, beloved one,
    My ev'ry joy hath flown;
I weep for thee, beloved one,
    I'm dreary, sad, alone.
            Thou art not here,
                    Dear love.

"As the last words died on my lips, I heard them, to my astonishment, repeated in the room which is closed; I heard plainly, clearly repeated the words 'Dear love,' and, Albert, it was the voice of your father; aye, start—you cannot feel as I felt at that moment: it was his clear, musical voice; I knew it in an instant, it vibrated through my nerves with the speed of the lightning, which was flashing vividly without. I listened with an intense anxiety to hear it repeated, the very pulsation of my heart was stilled in that moment; eagerly, earnestly did I bend every faculty to that one object, but in vain, I heard it not again."

"It was fancy, or the wind," interrupted Albert, whose feelings, in spite of himself, were strongly worked up by his mother's words.

" Peace, Albert, my story is yet to come," continued his mother solemnly. "Fancy! would to God it had been fancy, had been the wildest stretch of fancy which human imagination ever exercised; but no, Albert, it was too real; your father's bold spirit had imparted a portion of its courage to my woman's weakness, and, taking the light, I determined to enter the chamber and satisfy myself. As I was about to leave the room,

I turned and kissed your cheek; you smiled, and I offered up a prayer to the Almighty that you might live and prove a blessing to your parents; and I also offered one for your father's safety, when a sigh, a long, deep-drawn sigh, yet soft and low, sounded on my ear; it thrilled through me, freezing every drop of blood in my veins; for a moment I was motionless, I could not have moved although all the horrors of eternal torment had been the consequence of my remaining on that spot; yet I recovered myself, and, with a boldness I now wonder at, looked round, aye, searched the apartment for the cause; but I found nothing. I took the light in my hand, and descended the stairs; I entered the room from which I had heard the sound proceed; imagine my terror when the door closed behind me with a loud noise, a thunder-cloud burst, and crashed with frightful sound, the wind roared, the lightning flashed in long streams of fire, and, with the awful clamour which encircled me, the light dropped from my hand, and, for an instant, I was in total darkness—when, oh God! judge of my horror, I saw clearly, as distinctly as I see you now, Albert, your father—your father, pale to ashes, standing looking upon me. My blood crawled like ice through my veins, my flesh crept with a sensation of terror which was worse than death; he approached me; I could not move, I was rivetted to the ground, motionless, immoveable as if I had grown on the spot; he came nearer; I knew, Albert, I knew it was an apparition; he looked unearthly, his features were white as death and wan to misery from exhaustion and excessive fatigue; as he came close to me he smiled as only *he* could smile; he took my hand—Great Heaven! it was adding intense coldness to that which felt already ice; I could not breathe—I could not take my eyes from his, although I felt mine were living fire, and his were those of death; I did not faint—I did not expire. Why, I know not; yet I felt as though another minute of that feeling would be my destruction, when suddenly his voice broke upon my ear.

" ' Estelle,' he exclaimed, in the voice which was ever the sweetest music to me; ' Estelle, my dearly-loved Estelle, I see thee again, once again, for the last time: it is an awful trial, but the same Great Power which, in consideration of thine exceeding goodness, has granted this interview, will give you strength to bear it. I have but a few fleeting minutes to tell you this wondrous mystery; Estelle, I have not passed the boundary of death, nor have I the breath of human life in my nostrils; I cannot die—I do not live, as you exist, nor can I ever. Hear me: when I left you to seek the Indies for the wealth which was to enable me never again to leave you, I had determined my voyage should be as speedy as I could make it. I arrived at my destination, I sold my cargo, I realized a profit beyond my most sanguine expectations; the pleasure which this gave me made me long to regain my home; I longed to be with you, Estelle, never more to part. I had an indefinable dread of not accomplishing it; it preyed upon me, in spite of every effort I made to suppress it. We had a fair wind for home until we reached the Cape, then contrary winds prevailed: this I did not think much of at first, it was expected, still I tried to weather it but vainly; for nine long weeks did I sail round it without gaining ground; every impediment added to my anxiety to reach my port, still week after week passed away without obtaining my desire; the crew grew exhausted, yet I persevered. I carried every sail that would hold, but without avail; eighteen weeks passed, and still found me beating about the Cape. I grew frenzied, maddened; I swore almost unceasingly, raved, blasphemed; still my ship made no progress: I was requested to return to the Table Bay, but I stormed and swore I would persevere until I passed it. The crew, worn to skeletons with fatigue and excessive labour, came in a body, appealed to me as men who loved me, and would sail to the world's end, aye to death, cheerfully with me, to cease flying thus in the face of Providence, and return to the Bay until a favourable wind sprang up, or, at least, until the violence of the present storm abated. I refused; I called them by all the epithets my frantic rage brought to my tongue, and roared to them, that, come what might, I would persevere. The chief mate, whom, in my reasonable moments, I respected, and who, I believed, bore me all the affection one man can bestow upon another, turned to the crew and said he believed that I had lost my senses, that I was mad, and that it was their duty to bind me and take care of the ship and their own lives for me, if I would not myself, and he called to them to assist him in doing it; he advanced towards me, and seized me by the collar, while the crew prepared to follow, to carry his request into execution; but I disengaged myself from him, and struck him a violent blow upon the temple; he staggered with its violence, and at that moment a sudden squall threw the ship on her beam ends, he fell overboard, and sunk never to rise more. I then seized a capstan-bar, and, flourishing it to deter others from following his example, I swore by the Holy Virgin that I would pass the Cape in spite of storm, winds, fiends, hell, or Heaven itself, even if my doom were to beat about until the day of judgment. The words of that fearful oath had hardly passed my foaming lips, when a crash of thunder stunned every one on board; ere it had subsided we saw Peter Graat, the chief mate, standing in the midst of us; he fixed his eye upon me; I knew, I felt, he had come to pronounce judgment upon me for my terrible oath; he glared at me, and slowly raising his finger which he pointed to me, he opened his lips, and a hollow voice exclaimed—

" ' PHILIP VANDERDECKEN, YOU ARE DOOMED TO BEAT ABOUT UNTIL THE DAY OF JUDGMENT!'

" ' Estelle, that is my doom; there is one way of averting its duration. I have been permitted to see you, and in this sealed paper you will find the means; my time has passed—I leave you for ever. Estelle, best, dearest, — my own beloved Estelle, — we meet no more on earth.— Farewell!'

"I felt his hand leave mine; I saw his lineaments fading away; the room which, while *he* was there, seemed refulgent, was now clothed in darkness, and I was alone—alone, Albert. He whom I had loved, idolized, was thus torn from me for ever—for ever."

"Oh God!" burst forth Alfred, and he buried his face in his hands.

" Even in that awful darkness," continued the widow, "I knew I was alone. While he was there, I was in a state of stunned apathy; but when he went from me I screamed long and fainted. When I awoke from my swoon I beheld him, as I do now," shrieked the wretched Estelle,—" there, Albert," and she grasped his hand.

He started, as if he had been shot, from the position in which he was, and followed the direction of his mother's eyes with intense earnestness, but without encountering anything but vacancy. She pointed at some object, and with a voice which was almost screaming, cried,

"He is there, Albert—your father, Philip Vanderdecken. Look how his blue eye rests on you — he points at you, Albert; there now, at the room—Gracious God! he means—I see it all; he is leaving us. Philip, Philip, take me with you. Eighteen long years I have mourned you with tears and sighs—Philip, leave me not. I never smiled even at my boy's innocent prattle; I wept for you, Philip—will you not take me? He is passing away. Albert, stay him, it is your father! My first love, Philip, I come, I come—" and she sprang forwards as if to follow the object her distempered imagination had conjured up, and Albert, who had been paralysed by the suddenness of her frenzy and by the fearful history she had just related, had scarcely time to spring after her, reach her, and catch her in his arms as she was falling.

"Mother, mother," was all he could exclaim, his heart was full to bursting. He lifted her gently, and carried her to her chair, but she was dead.

CHAPTER II.

A MISER, A PRIEST, A ROBBERY, AND A CHASE.

ALBERT used every means he could think of for several minutes to restore his mother, but not finding any signs of life he grew dreadfully alarmed; he ran out of the house and battered at the door of the next house as though he intended to break it down; the violence of his knocking soon brought its inmates to the door, to ascertain the cause of the clatter, and there they beheld Albert without his hat, a face full of distraction, and heard him exclaim, "My mother—my mother," as he pointed to the door of his mother's house: in another minute he darted from them at his utmost speed, and was out out of sight; the alarmed neighbours entered the house and saw the widow Vanderdecken in the chair, in the position in which Albert had placed her. They carried her to bed, applied vainly every remedy which came to their recollection or means, to restore to life one whom life had quitted for ever.

About a mile and a half from the residence of Albert Vanderdecken was the habitation of one of the most miserable, wretched, miserly, little doctors in all Holland, Winken Kroots; the house was not of very vast extent, but it was snug enough in its appearance; the lower windows were barred, and the upper ones were closed by shutters of strong make; the door was of stout oak, and of such make that it seemed to defy all efforts which might be made to burst it open, should any occasion require such a forcible mode of entry: the house did not look, certainly, like the residence of a doctor, to which it is supposed that all persons have at all times free egress, except in these cut and curtailing hours of business times,

when all persons are to be kept out of places of business after eight o'clock, and invited to those places of *amusement* which they should not go in, at all hours of the night, and all for the advance of knowledge and morality. Winken Kroots was at home compounding drugs and calculating his gains, running through his daily expenses, and cudgelling his brain to hit upon some article which he could dispense with to decrease his expense and increase his income; it was a matter of some difficulty to him, he having already reduced his household expenses to as small a sum as could be, and therefore it was to little purpose that he followed the idea; he gave it up at last, and trusted that fortune would send him some new patient, out of whom he might get enough extra profit to counterbalance the failure of the desired saving. While deeply engaged in this reverie, a knock came at the door, which made him jump as a kitten does when suddenly startled, all four legs off the ground at once. Now though it is not meant to be insinuated that Winken Kroots had four legs—indeed the two he had were particularly shrivelled and thin,—yet we affirm that he jumped off the ground a matter of ten inches when that tremendous loud knock came, and his heart beat almost as loud, and certainly as fast, although the knocks at the door rained as swift as a stalwart pair of arms could direct them. Winken Kroots paused, he had always a kind of alarm hanging over him —he had cause; he had money—he loved it dearly; and there were people, he knew, roaming about who, if they became aware of its existence in Winken Kroots' house, would not have remembered the eighth commandment; besides, they were not troubled by conscience. Winken Kroots, as we have said, knew this fact, and therefore, when this violent knocking took place, he naturally remembered violent marauders, and consequently his money; he therefore paused.

" Winken Kroots, Winken Kroots !" shouted a voice outside the door. "Whose voice can that be?" wondered Winken Kroots, " for I am sure I have heard it before."

" Winken Kroots, Winken Kroots !" roared the voice, " open the door, open the door, I say; am I to stand here knocking and roaring while life and death is in my errand ?"

" Why that's Albert Vanderdecken's voice, I delare," thought Kroots, " the most passionate, hasty dog in Amsterdam, and one of the poorest."

" Hear me, Kroots," roared Albert, in a passion, " I know you are at home, and if you don't come out I'll break down your door and drag you with me, if it's by the neck; open, I say, open," and he redoubled his knocks at the door.

" One of the poorest;" ejaculated Kroots, " don't be in such a violent hurry, Master Vanderdecken," answered he in a loud voice, " I am en-, gaged, an cannot attend to you just now."

" But you shall," bawled Albert in a towering rage; " you must, Kroots. Winken Kroots, my mother is dying—may be dead while I am standing here—come out, or I'll murder you in another minute if you keep me here."—and out of excess of passion he redoubled his blows on the door.

" One of the poorest," muttered Kroots, and proceeded to unbar and open the door; before the last bolt had been drawn back a second, he found himself in the clutches of Albert, and being shook with a violence which gave credit to Vanderdecken's muscles.

" You little miserable wretch," cried Albert, with a face as red as fire, and the tears standing like large pearls in his eyes; " you little varlet, my mother is dangerously ill, suddenly attacked; come with me this instant, or I'll be the death of you;" and he proceeded to drag Winken Kroots along with him; the latter, however, struggled and kicked. " Hands off," he cried, " hands off, Mynheer Vanderdecken; what, do you mean to be the death of me ?"

" Yes," exclaimed Albert as he gave him a parting shake, " yes; unless you come at once."

" Have you the money to spare, Master Albert; I cannot give my attendance for nothing, I should starve if I did, for I am very poor—very poor."

" What do you mean," roared Albert.

" Two guilders," meekly replied Kroots.

" Look you, Winken Kroots—you know me, you know Albert Vanderdecken never broke his word; now listen, for I speak not again, if you do not come with me at once I will strangle you on the spot; but as I do not wish to have murder on my soul I advise you to come at once and quietly; but I have no dishonesty in my character, and you shall be paid, if I sell the last thing I have in the world to meet your demand, be it what it may, so come along."

" Yes, but I shall have to wait for my money, and at ten per cent. interest," said Kroots, " that will make——"

" You miserly little wretch, kindness is lost upon you," exclaimed Albert; and he seized Winken Kroots by the collar, and dragged him in the direction of his mother's cottage with all the force he was master of.

" Murder, help !" roared Kroots. " I will come; let me go, good Master Albert, you are choking me."

Albert judged, by the sound emitted from the throat of Kroots, that there was some truth in the remark; he therefore quitted his hold, and restored the little man to his equilibrium.

" There," he exclaimed; " now, sir, you can judge of what I will do."

" Oh dear," cried little Kroots, rubbing his neck and coughing with his eyes full of water, " oh dear ! I had nearly given up the ghost; I will come; you have promised to pay me, and you always keep your word; I will but get my hat and stick, and then I will attend you."

" Kroots, you will wear my patience threadbare; come along without it," hallooed Albert in a voice of thunder. " I tell you, you shall have your money, if I part with my dress to pay you; come, tarry another moment if you wish to lose your life."

" I am with you, then," said Kroots. " Patience, quotha," he muttered as he complied with the request of Albert, and both proceeded at a rapid pace to Vanderdecken's house.

They soon arrived there, and found the neighbours surrounding the bed upon which they had laid the Widow Vanderdecken. Albert hastily broke through them, dragging Kroots with him : he looked wildly at his mother; her face, which was always pale, had now assumed a ghastly whiteness, which made him shudder as he gazed upon it; the fallen jaw also caught his sight, and, pressing his hands upon his eyes, he cried—

" Look, Kroots, she is there; tell me the worst, is she—is my mother live ?"

" No," replied Kroots, " she is dead."

" I thought so," groaned Albert; " God rest thy soul, my blessed, lessed mother," and he flung himself by her side on the bed.

The neighbours who witnessed the act, with a delicacy which did onour to their feelings, retired, and left Kroots alone with Albert.

Albert, absorbed in grief, thought of all his mother had said in their last interview; he shuddered as he reflected on what he had heard, and of its consequences to her.

Mynheer Kroots thought of his guilders, of the possibility of obtaining them, and he cast his eyes anxiously round the room with the intention of discovering if there was anything which would indemnify him for his bill, providing the money was not forthcoming. As various articles of furniture caught his eye, he estimated their value, and found that there would be more than enough to satisfy his bill, were it forty times as heavy; but then he calculated upon the time which might elapse ere Albert would sell the articles, if indeed he parted with them at all; in such a case, how was he to get his money ? Now, if there was some small article which he could accept in lieu of coin, some little thing worth treble his demand, he would be satisfied; his small but sharp black eyes were cast round the room in search of some such desideratum, and they performed the circuit of it without coming to a successful conclusion, until they alighted upon the corpse; they rested for a moment—they were attracted by a glittering ornament upon the neck; what could that be? it was a relic—a portion of the true and Holy Cross set in richly chased silver and jewels; its value as a relic was considerable, but the setting was of much greater. Kroots, who was skilled in the knowledge of those things, detected its worth in a second; he approached the body—Albert stirred not; he took up the relic, it was fastened to a thin but exquisitely worked gold chain—still Albert was motionless; the chain was clasped with an ornament studded with small diamonds; Kroots's eyes sparkled as he looked upon it—his mouth watered: if he received this in payment, what an enormous profit he should clear. He looked at Albert, he appeared perfectly unconscious of everything around him; he unclasped the chain with trembling fingers—the relic was in his hands—in his pocket. He drew a long breath; Albert had not witnessed the transaction; of that he was sure, he therefore, with some exertion of courage, tapped him on the shoulder and exclaimed,

"Mynheer Vanderdecken, I must leave you; I can do no good here, your mother is dead, and quite beyond the reach of my skill; you will pay me my bill that you promised me, I must go now, I have a patient to visit."

"Go!" replied Albert, who had not raised his head.

"Very well, could not you pay me now?" asked Kroots.

"No," returned Albert,

"Can you give me anything in exchange? I will take anything that will cover the amount of my charge, after deducting the expense of selling it."

"Go," thundered Albert.

"I will," returned Kroots, "but you recollect my charge is two guilders; you know, if I come again, it will cost you another, because I cannot give my time, you understand; you will pay me, Mynheer Vanderdecken, you have passed your word that you will."

"Leave the house, you miserly little rat!" roared Albert, springing from the bed in an extacy of passion; "you shall have your paltry demand, I have given my word and I never break it, so leave me or I will shake you to death." So concluding he took Winken Kroots by the shoulders, and thrust him violently forth from the house.

Albert was now alone with the body of his mother—his mother whom he had so dearly loved, the only being whom he had known to have loved him, the only one he had ever loved, taken from him under such awful circumstances, even while the words of that dreadful sentence were on her lips; his head throbbed violently, his eyes were hot and bloodshot, and he felt as if his heart would break, yet no tear came to his relief. It was that agonizing grief which scorches the frame, and a flood of tears would have brought him the same relief which a refreshing rain does to the parched earth, but they were denied to him, and he groaned with an agony of feeling as he pressed his hands to his hot and throbbing temples; in this state he remained without moving for several hours. At last he partially recovered himself, and walked to the side of the bed which contained the remains of his mother, he gazed upon her face which had now, despite the circumstances under which she had breathed her last, and the rigidity which death produces, assumed the appearance of calm placidity. He kissed her cold forehead, and, kneeling down by her side, offered up with fervour, prayers for her repose.

"Spirit of my sainted mother," he concluded, "watch over me and breathe the influence of thy gentle spirit and of thy goodness over my actions, that when my hour arrives to quit this earth, my spirit may rejoin thine, and——" here he paused and bowed his head, which, in his earnestness had been upturned, lowly and humbly, as the recollection of his father's doom flashed across his mind; he shuddered as he reflected on the terrible punishment which was to endure until the day of judgment; then he remembered his mother had mentioned there were means of averting the duration of the punishment, but how? Was he to be the instrument?—it must be so, but what the means? "Ah! the sealed packet," he cried, as the thought struck him, "which my father gave my mother on his mysterious appearance, that must contain the directions; where has my mother placed it? Has it left the room in which it was brought, or does it still remain there?"—he determined to search the apartment.

Albert possessed a great amount of moral courage; ordinary dangers were of little import to him, in point of effect upon his mind, and no man possessed less superstition than himself; yet he could not help feeling an unaccountable awe steal over him—an indefinable dread, as he came to the determination of searching that closed apartment, the room which God's light had not penetrated for eighteen years. Still it was a duty—a painful, fearful one, it was true; but it must be fulfilled, and he was not one to shrink from a path which he deemed it right he should pursue, and this was one which he felt himself bound by every circumstance to investigate. Could it be the influence of a diseased imagination acting upon a weak constitution, and upon a mind strained to the utmost in the sickness of expectation, which had produced a delusion to the brain of his mother, or was it REALITY? He was torn by conflicting thoughts; there was something so incredible in his mother's dreadful narrative, that his mind a thousand times rejected the belief, yet his father had never returned— been heard of, and it had produced his mother's death. This terrible uncertainty distracted him, and his nature was not such, that where there was a possibility of satisfying a doubt, to remain long in the dark respecting it; he therefore resolved that at once he would set his doubts at rest by an immediate investigation of the room, and he had but to get the key, and a few minutes would decide the truth or falsity of the appearance of his father. The key had been taken from the door on the morning after the mysterious occurrence, and placed in some secret spot by his mother; he had therefore to search for it, as he never knew where she had placed it. There was an antique cabinet filled with drawers standing in the room he was in, which contained various articles belonging to his mother; he had never, to his recollection, seen it open, and it was the first which recurred to his memory, as the most probable place to contain the key. He went to it, unlocked it, and opened drawer after drawer without discovering the object of his search; he took every drawer out, and went carefully through all the various articles to prevent missing it, had it chanced to have slipped between them. He came to the last drawer, he opened it, and found nothing but a letter in it: he was about to close it with a motion of angry disappointment, when the superscription of the letter caught his eye: it was thus addressed—

"To whoever, in the event of my sudden death, shall become possessed of my effects, and this house.

ESTELLE VANDERDECKEN."

Albert snatched it up and read it several times to assure himself that it was real; it was in his mother's handwriting, "and now," thought he, as he broke the seal with trembling but eager fingers, "I shall know my course:" he opened it and read :—

"Almighty Father, to thee I commit myself, thy ways are inscrutable, and though my future existence may and will be unto me a living death, I bow myself to thy will, and bear thy dispensation with meekness and resignation, until the hour arrives when it shall please thee, O my Father, to call me unto thyself.

"An awful and mysterious event has befallen me, so terrible that I can scarcely command my mind to write these few lines; it is an event which concerns me and my child only. Should I not reveal it to him, ere I breathe my last sigh, it will die with me. That which occurred took place in the room which has been closed, and will remain so until I am a tenant of the grave: in that room, upon the table, is a sealed packet; in the event of its not coming into the possession of my son, let the priest destroy it, for it is an accursed and unholy thing. Should my son obtain it, let him reflect ere he opens it. He will know all that I know, and will not that knowledge be enough without searching deeper ?—too much, too much! On removing this drawer from its case, and placing the hand in the right hand corner, a spring of a secret drawer will be discovered—in that drawer rests the key of the room, where the cold, glazed, blue eyes fixed their deathly glance on mine, as now—there,— see——"

The succeeding words were illegible, as though her mind had wandered while committing the last lines to the paper, and mournfully did Albert recall to his memory many times in former years when he had seen his mother labouring under the influence of this mental agony, While lost in this sad reflection, a knocking at the door occurred; he aroused with a start, and hastily folding the letter, he hid it in his vest, and went to the door to demand the cause of the knocking; on opening it, he beheld the priest, Father Francis, his mother's confessor, standing before him.

"The blessing of the Holy Virgin be upon you, my son," said the father in a soft, mild tone; "I have been informed thy mother is at the last extremity, and I am here to offer her that spiritual comfort and consolation which is the stay and support of those who die in the true faith."

Albert crossed himself devoutly as he received the blessing of Fathe

Francis, and replied:—" Most holy father, my mother is with the blessed."

" Dead !" ejaculated the father in a voice of surprise.

" Dead," responded Albert, and bowed his head with anguish.

" And her spirit has passed away without receiving the rites of our Holy Church," said Father Francis, in a tone of reproof. " Son, this is a fault; why was not a messenger sent unto me ?"

" Father, she died even while in converse with me," replied Albert; " she became agitated with violent emotion at the subject of our conversation, and the excitement proved too great for her weakness; she swooned, as I thought, and leaving her to the care of neighbours, I ran for Winken Kroots, and on my return with him, I found her swoon was that of death."

" May the blessed Virgin receive her," prayed Father Francis.

" Amen," responded Albert as he crossed himself. " Good father," he continued, " will you not see her ere you depart ?"

With a motion of assent the father followed Albert to the apartment which contained his mother's remains, and when he reached the bedside he gazed for a few minutes upon the deceased widow, then sprinkling the bed with holy water, he knelt down and prayed.

Albert gazed on the good man as he humbly bent in prayer, and upon his dear mother as she lay in the calm, tranquil sleep of death, and for the first time tears came to his relief; he clasped his hands convulsively together, then pressed them to his eyes; his whole frame shook with the intensity of his emotion, and large tears came trickling through his fingers; for a minute he gave way to its power, and sobbed like a child, but, like the heavy rain from a thunder cloud, it passed away as rapidly as it came, and when Father Francis had risen to his feet, Albert's eyes were as dry as dust again. The father turned his eyes upon him, for he had heard him sob, with the intention of offering him consolation, but he saw with surprise the drawers of the cabinet strewn over the apartment, while their contents were thrown about exhibiting the greatest disorder: as he witnessed this, his countenance gradually became stern, and he said with a severity of tone,

" Son, son, this is most unseemly, it is very wrong, even unfeeling; thy mother's spirit hath scarcely left its mortal tenement, ere thou art counting thine earthly gain; for shame ! this is wicked."

" Do not judge me so harshly, holy father," repled Albert deprecatingly " There is a secret of a terrible nature, which was between my sainted mother and myself; it is connected with that closed room, and I but sought the key to solve a mystery which I cannot endure—a suspense which would, if not set at rest, drive me mad."

" What is the secret ?—will you not trust it with me ?" asked Father Francis, I feel it must be of some extraordinary nature to have induced you to violate the appearance of decency; for I know, my son, you loved your mother."

" I did, I did," groaned Albert.

" Confide in me," continued the good father, " I am old; my experience is vast, and I may, by my spiritual assistance, grant you that peace of mind which the posession of a terrible secret always denies to the holder."

" Good Father," returned Albert, " I know your motive is a high and good one ; from my soul I thank you for it, but I cannot reveal the secret, at least at present ; there is still a portion of it to be learned ; if I should obtain that, and should feel it would be right to disclose it, I will repose my confidence in you ; till then, my own bosom must be the depositary of my secret."

" Be it as you will," said Father Philip, " if you feel you ought not disclose it ; I will not desire you to make it known ; indeed I believe you to be right, and give you credit for your firmness ; for your mother, when at confession, told me there was a mystery connected with that chamber, but would not confess its nature ; she believed herself to be ful- filling a duty, and she was a good and holy woman ; therefore, when the time arrives which may induce you to confide in me, I trust it will be in my power to assist you with my counsel and my prayers ; my blessing upon you, my son."

Albert bowed his head, and the good father blessed him, and walked slowly and sadly away.

A few days elapsed, and the Widow Vanderdecken was sleeping in her grave, with the green turf above her. Albert was now alone in the world ; the only relative he knew himself to possess was his mother's brother, and he was the captain of a vessel, one who trod the shore little, and had seen his sister and her child less. Albert, therefore, thought not about him, and felt himself alone ; it was a sad feeling, yet, with a temper like his, it had the effect of consolation ; it led him to depend on his own resources ; he looked around him, and knew no human being whom he could call friend, he had none ; he had made none ; yet he had many acquaintances, and all who knew him felt a kind and friendly feeling towards him ; but he had kept them at a distance, not from any idea that they were not equal to him in society, but from a strong feeling of pride, which sensitive minds always possess upon certain points. His mother and himself were poor—very poor ; but it cost him little reflection to perceive that she had not always been so : the house in which they lived was his mother's property ; it had been built, decorated, and furnished, with that attention to comforts, and even luxury, which a well-stocked purse commands. The neighbours did not, although they were aware the widow's circumstances were straitened, know their poverty was so great as it really was ; for her brother occasionally sent her small sums, which were eked out, with all the economy possible ; their wants were few, and easily satisfied. Albert was therefore desirous that those persons who had known them in their better days should not now come in to spy the nakedness of the land : this feeling had induced him to shrink from anything like intimacy with his neighbours ; his mother's society had been all in all to him ; now she was taken from him he felt a sensation of loneliness which made the world seem a desert to him. He had mixed with the young men of the neighbourhood as a lord among his vassals ; he had joined their sports and enterprises with an energy, and high reckless daring, which startled even the boldest among them : he was the victor in all their sports, and the leader in any wild or dangerous enter- prises in which they engaged : he was the chief among them—felt, acted, and was treated as such ; he ever received the profoundest respect ; he

Struggle between Vanderdecken and Winken Kroots.

commanded it by his superior bearing, and by his conduct; his word once passed was never broken; and in all disputes among the young men he was referred to as judge, and his decision was accepted as final. His impartiality and love of truth had obtained this deference for him, but it had kept him aloof, and prevented him forming a friendship with those whom he felt were inferior to him in spirit and moral courage. No real friendship can exist where there is not a mutual sympathy: Albert felt this, and would not waste his best feelings upon one uncongenial to his taste.

He had, as has been told, determined to search the apartment which had remained for so long a period unopened; and, having discovered the key in the spot where his mother had directed him in her letter, he, on the morning after his mother's interment, resolved to enter the room; as he was about to fulfil his intention, he was disturbed by a knocking without, and, upon opening the door, Winken Kroots trotted in.

"Good morning, Mynheer Vanderdecken," he exclaimed, "I hope you have recovered your loss; we must all die, eh? sometime or other; but we must also live, eh? you understand?"

"To what do you allude?" asked Albert, gloomily, for his mind was excited by the task he was about to undertake, and the presence of the little doctor added to his depression.

No. 3.   D.

" Oh," cried Winken, as if the other could not misunderstand so evident an allusion, " Oh, Mynheer Albert, when I say we must all live, I mean, that while we exist, we must do the best we can to prevent our starving; eh?"

" Well," ejaculated Albert.

" And—and so—I—you see," the little doctor hesitated; Albert's previous roughness had alarmed him.

" Go on," cried Albert, raising his voice, and frowning.

" I am very poor, very, very poor," replied Kroots, making an adverb of the adjective, and speaking rather quickly; " and you know you promised to pay me, and you have the reputation of never breaking your word."

" You will find it truth," replied Albert, "you shall have your money; I have said it, that is enough."

" Why no," returned Winken, " not quite enough, I want the money; you say I shall have it, but when, when, eh? Mynheer Vanderdecken? you know that "while the grass grows the steed starves," using the proverb which was an old one in Hamlet's time.

" Look you," returned Albert, " I have told you that you shall be paid; it does not suit me just now to do so; but, to show you I mean the truth, were it the last thing I had in the world I would part with it, rather than you should not be paid your wretched trifle; now leave me, for I am not in the humour to stand parleying with you upon a subject such as this."

" But, Mynheer Vanderdecken," returned the little impersonation of miserly misery, anxiously, " you can give me something in lieu; you have plenty of things, I am not particular; I want no large piece of furniture; no, some small trinket, some little valuable of your mother's, which is of no use to you, that little piece of the Holy Cross, which she wore round her neck—now I should—"

" Winken Kroots," roared Albert, interrupting him with a voice of thunder, " if you would not have me break every bone in that most wretched little carcase of thine you will depart instantly, and without another word."

" Will you not let me have the relic?" asked Kroots with much anxiety.

" No," thundered Albert, whose passion was getting to a stormy height, " No, you epitome of avarice, no! not if you offered me fifty thousand guilders, and every guilder was equal to a million, I would not part with it; and now take my word, if you do not depart while I have command of my temper, you will never reach your home alive; begone!" And he slammed the door with such violence, that Winken, who had been standing upon the threshold, received a severe blow upon his forehead and nose, lost his equilibrium, and discovered himself, half stunned, seated upon the ground: he got up, he did not like having possession of the relic; but his fear of Albert's passion, when he should discover that he had taken it, and, added to that, the great dislike he felt in parting with so valuable an ornament, which he held for so small a sum, determined him to walk home, and wait a little while, to see what would occur; accordingly he traced his way home. Albert, when Winken had left him, bestowed a few epithets on the intruder, and his avarice; in the chain of ideas which followed, he thought of the relic which he had known his mother to have set such store by; he immediately began to conjecture where it was: till this moment he had forgotten it; he ran up into the room where his mother had laid, he looked every where, but in vain; 'twas not there; where could it be? It had never been buried with his mother; impossible! how had Winken Kroots known that his mother possessed such an article? "Ah!" a thought struck him; he remembered the conversation which had taken place between himself and Kroots at the bed-side, where his mother lay dead. "The wretch has taken it, stolen it, robbed it from my mother's neck, even while I was by her side; but I will have it; he left here but a minute since; that was his anxiety, was it? he shall restore it, if I crush him to atoms." In another instant, Albert was at the top of his speed on the track of Winken Kroots.

Winken Kroots was on his road home, as we have already stated; Winken felt uneasy; he was a misèr, back and edge; he would swindle, extort, rob, in fact do anything for money; he had an amazing amount of rascality, but no courage; his was not daring villany; it was miserable wickedness; an inordinate, insatiate covetousness, which suffered no sin, even of the worst kind, to interfere with the gratification of his adoration for gold; he had no religion, but he had conscience—something too much for his comfort, it pricked, and stirred him up uncommonly; it was not the fear of a future world, of a future frying for his crimes in this world; it was the horrid fear that he should be unlucky enough to be hauled over the coals here—he let the hereafter take care of itself—for one of his little aggressions of the law of justice. In the case of the abstraction of the relic from the neck of the widow Vanderdecken, he knew he had committed a breach of the laws, which made him liable to a severe punishment. If Albert should discover his loss, and proceed to extremities, he should be in a most disagreeable situation; have all his property confiscated, and probably his life would be forfeited; the laws in Holland, in 1640, were very severe; they had need be, for there was a great deal of robbery going on at that time. Winken cogitated upon his situation, when a distant hallo broke upon his ear; ere he turned his head, with a speed which surpasses all description the thoughts were through his brain that Albert had missed the cross, suspected him, had come after him, and that hallo was intended to stop him: he looked round; it was Albert, tearing, flying along; Winken's heart beat fast, he was alarmed. Albert was terribly hasty and passionate; Winken got very frightened; Albert had threatened to murder him—if he should keep his word—Winken broke out in a cold sweat; his house was not far off; if he could gain it before Albert overtook him, he could parley with him, with the door between them, without much damage being done; his street door was an oak door, very remarkably strong; "Holloa!" shouted the voice much nearer to him; Albert was coming up rapidly; in an agony of fear off darted Winken. "Ah! wretch!" sounded in his ear; it lent him speed; Winken's little legs went over much ground in little time; it was remarkable to see how he used them—to see how he held his little head and neck between his shoulders; he went very fast, but Albert, in all matches of speed with his neighbours, in which he had been engaged, came off victorious. In the present case, he flew along with a swiftness almost incredible; the very act of Winken's running had proved to him that he had got the relic; and it roused his ire to such a degree that he had serious thoughts of tearing him to pieces, and scattering him unto the four winds of heaven like a handful of feathers. Winken had some such horrid idea also of his fate, unless he escaped the fangs of his pursuer; the fright of such a termination to his existence lent him wings; his little legs rattled along like drum-sticks beating a roll call. Away they went, pursuer and pursued: the odds were in favour of Albert, who was gaining fast on Winken—they were both aware of that fact; still less grew the distance between them—they each redoubled their speed—Albert occasionally roaring out an epithet with the utmost bitterness, as well as his breath would permit him: ". Wretch! miserable dog! Rogue, I have thee, I'll tear thy wretched heart out." These broken words were all heard by Winken, who increased his exertions with every endeavour he was master of; every word Albert uttered sounded at a less distance, and one cry from Albert of " Aha! dog, you are mine," came close to his ears, he felt the tips of Albert's fingers scratching down his back, then he bounded, and shrieked in the extremity of his terror; his door was within a few yards of him, his flight became now a series of bounds, of leaps; he yelled; his door was open; again Albert's fingers were on his shoulders; again he shrieked and leaped; he gained the door, he dashed in, and in another second they were rolling on the floor together, but Winken Kroots was up like a shot, and darted up a flight of stairs, followed so close by Albert, that he felt him grasping at his legs, he lifted them up as though he was upon red-hot iron; he gained the top; so did Albert; they both dashed into a room together, and again they both came violently to the ground—but this time Albert had firm hold of the wretched little doctor, and was proceeding to twist his neck, in the violence of his rage, when a voice cried, " Hold !"

He turned round hastily, for the word was uttered in a clear musical voice, but yet so commandingly, that he unconsciously obeyed it, and beheld a female standing over him; he gazed upon her with astonishment; her beauty was transcendant, it quite overcame his faculties; and, quitting his hold of Kroots, he rose from the ground with his eyes still fixed earnestly upon her; was it enchantment that one so surpassingly lovely should have thus become suddenly visible in the house of the wretched Kroots? Who could she be? No relative of Kroots; there could be no doubt of that; whence did she spring? Albert had frequently been in the residence of Kroots, had passed it at all times, and at all hours, and had never seen even the seventy-seventh shadow of a shade of a female in the habitation: and now, one with a presence of dazzling beauty, springs in to being at a moment of deadly strife; it was strange! Albert could not withdraw his eyes from the maiden; she was evidently of eastern origin; her full dark eyes in their quiescent state beamed with love and tenderness; but could flash a fire fierce as the vivid lightning, when roused into action; her nose was thin and straight, her lips red, and delicately small, her eyebrows were beautifully curved, and her eye-lashes exquisitely pencilled, giving a dreaminess to the eyes beyond all description beautiful:

> " See where she stands ! a mortal shape endued,
>   With love and life and light and deity,
>   And motion, which may change but cannot die—
>   An image of some bright eternity;
>   A shadow of some golden dream ; a splendour
>   Leaving the third sphere pilotless ; a tender
>   Reflection of the eternal moon of love,
>   Under whose motions life's dull billows move ;
>   A metaphor of spring, and youth, and morning ;
>   A vision like incarnate April, warning,
>   With smiles and tears, Frost the anatomy
>   Into his summer grave."

Albert was fascinated, rooted to the spot, his eyes had never beheld any female half so enchanting ; and it was not until he heard the voice of the maiden demanding the cause of his intrusion, and saw the blush mantling her cheek, that he was conscious that his prolonged and ardent gaze must be distressing ; he recovered himself, and, bowing, said :

" This violent intrusion must appear extraordinary on my part, but, when I have explained the cause, you will acknowledge, maiden, that I was justified in my conduct."

" It must have been something of a shocking nature to have induced you to attempt a murder," replied the lady.

Albert started when he heard his conduct thus denominated, and Winken Kroots groaned.

" Murder," echoed Albert, " Murder—I fear that but for your timely interruption, Winken Kroots would not have been of this world at this moment."

Again Winken groaned.

" What act of my father's could have justified so violent a proceeding ?" demanded the maiden.

" Winken Kroots your father ; impossible !" ejaculated Albert.

" The possibility of such a circumstance can have no connexion with my question," returned the female.

" True—but it cannot be ; nothing should induce me to believe it," exclaimed Albert, as he looked at Winken Kroots with an expression of utter scorn, and then returned his eyes to the lady with a glance of an exactly opposite character. " Maiden," he said, " this man I employed to attend my mother, who was suddenly stricken with death while in my arms, although I knew it not at the time ; and while she lay dead upon her bed, and I, absorbed in an agony of grief, had flung myself by her side, this wretch, this miserly villain, robbed my sainted mother's body of a relic, a portion of the true and Holy Cross, which has been in our family for several hundred years, even while I was kneeling at the bed side."

" Good Heaven ! is this true ?" cried the maiden.

" No ! Aylmine ; no !" muttered Koots.

" No !" exclaimed Albert. " Liar, thou hast it ; and if I have it not returned to me at once, tremble, thou vile wretch, for thy safety."

" You need use no violence, sir," said the lady, " you are too rash and impetuous. Father, restore the youth his property at once; it is not thine, therefore return it to him."

" But what security shall I have for the money he owes me, if I give it up ?" replied Kroots, forgetting, in his anxiety for payment, that he acknowledged the possession of the property.

" Then you have taken it !" exclaimed Aylmine.

" I told you so—I knew he had ;" said Albert.

" I merely took it as an equivalent, as security," mumbled Kroots.

" Wretch !" ejaculated Albert.

" Restore it, father, instantly ; it is a monstrous, wicked act," said the female, and advanced to the little doctor, who had risen from the ground the instant Albert had quitted his hold, and retreated, panting, to a chair at the extremity of the room.

"But Aylmine, my child, I am poor.   Mynheer Vanderdecken owes me money," said Kroots, showing horrible reluctance to return Albert the relic.

" Every farthing of which shall be paid, Winken Kroots," said Albert, with a flush on his brow ; " have I not passed my word that I will do so, and when was Albert Vanderdecken ever known to break it ?"

" Where is the relic, father ?" asked Aylmine, while the blood tinged on her cheeks and forehead at her father's disgraceful conduct, " Give it me," she said, imperatively.   " Oh, it is a most dishonourable, a most mean action !"

Her power seemed great over the little miser, for he drew forth the relic from his bosom to restore it, but when its glittering form caught his eyes, it seemed an impossibility to him to part with it ; it was too much for his weak nerves, and he was about to return it to his breast again ; but the hand of Aylmine was already upon the chain, and the next instant Albert was crossing himself, and pressing the holy thing to his lips with the utmost reverence.

" Now, lady, let me humbly thank you for your service, and beg your forgiveness for my hasty and rude conduct ; but this relic belonged to my dear, dear mother, who is now with the blessed ; she prized it beyond anything she possessed in the world, and I—leaving my religious veneration for it out of the question—value it as highly, for it was a thing which she loved."

" I acquit you, sir," returned Aylmine, " fully ; your conduct was justified by its cause."

" I thank you, lady," replied Albert, " and now I have my property restored, my animosity has ceased ; Kroots, I forgive you ; lady, farewell— when next we meet, I trust it will be in a more pleasing way," he bowed, and prepared to depart.

"But you will pay me, Mynheer Vanderdecken," cried Kroots.

" Father !" said Aylmine, reproachfully,

"In three days at farthest," returned Albert, "you shall have four guilders, Winken Kroots."

Winken rubbed his hands.

Albert turned to Aylmine, their eyes met, and Albert felt a sudden but pleasing shock thrill every nerve in his body ; he bowed low, and descended the stairs.

" She is very beautiful," thought he, as he quitted the house ; he walked homeward, musingly.

" Three days?" he exclaimed, as he nearly reached his home, " I can surely call and pay Winken Kroots in less than three days !"

CHAP. III.

THE OPENING OF THE CLOSED CHAMBER.　THE SEALED PACKET.

Albert had determined to open the chamber, when he was so suddenly prevented by the circumstances narrated in the last chapter; and when he returned home he was wearied with the excitement of the chase, and his head was full of thoughts of the beautiful Aylmine; he was in no frame of mind to enter on such an investigation as the searching of that mysterious chamber, and he therefore resolved to wait until the following morning ere he proceeded on it. The next morning came; a most lovely one; a beautiful warm morning in the middle of 'sweet May,' the loveliest month in the year; the sky was pale blue, growing paler as it reached the horizon; no cloud obscured the sun's brilliancy, all nature seemed redolent with light; the flowers and the green trees revelled in freshness and beauty; birds were flying here and there, warbling as though their little throats would burst with delight; a light cool wind played in the air, modifying the heat gratefully; it was a beautiful sunny morning, casting a gladness over every thing; yet it had a depressing influence upon Albert; it formed so strong a contrast to the task he was about to undertake, that he wished the morning had been less bright; a dull cloudy obscure morning would have suited his purpose better; he hesitated whether he should not wait; yet the suspense—that was dreadful—he could not endure it; "besides," he thought, what have I to fear; fear—nonsense—it is not that—but there is a strange awe creeps over me when I think of that room; why should there be ?— I have done no wrong; whatever may be in that room cannot harm me; there can only be evidence of the truth or falsity of what my mother has communicated to me;—why then should I hesitate ? still I feel that room is connected with my destiny."

" Thy destiny !" exclaimed a hollow voice.

Albert started violently, and felt a chill run through his veins; he looked around him, but nothing was visible; he was in a room on the ground floor —and next to the one he was about to search—the door was closed; the voice sounded close to his ear, he had turned with the speed of lightning to the spot from which it had proceeded, but he could see nothing more than usual; he was the only living thing in the room; this event, which would have cowed the hearts of most persons, had the effect of strengthen-ing his resolution, and hastening his proceedings. " It is strange," he muttered, " but I must and will see the end of it all." The key was in his hand and he left the room, and arrived in a minute at the door of the chamber, which was now to be opened for the first time after a lapse of eighteen years since the events of that terrible night, which Albert's mother had met her death in relating; he put the key in the lock and turned it; as the bolt flew back he felt cold and sick with excitement; but, drawing a long breath, he threw the door open, with a strange horrid, expectation of seeing some one start out; but no, all was still as death, and as dark; he stood upon the threshold, and looked into the darkness as if he would penetrate every corner of the room ere he crossed the threshold; as he gazed earnestly before him he saw a round white object

—it was apparently higher than he stood by two or *th*ree feet—he looked at it to endeavour to make it out; he took a step into the room; he stared hard, peered anxiously at it; his eyes were growing familiar to the darkness, and the open door of the room communicated a small portion of light, although it was situated in a dark passage leading to the street door. Albert began to see the white object take a form—he made out a pair of blue eyes—they soon became clear and distinct. Good God! he had heard his mother speak of his father's blue eyes; he now saw them as plain as if the room had been full of light; he made out the rest of the features plainly, it seemed a counterpart of himself; he felt his blood turn cold, he stared at it as if his eyes would start from their sockets, and the face—the eyes were turned on him with a calm placid gaze. Albert felt rooted to the spot; he felt a sensation of awe—of agony creeping, crawling over him; he buried his face in his hands to shut it out from his sight; but felt impelled again to look: it was as though some power irresistible was tearing his hands down to make him look on that face; his hands fell to his side, and still was the face there looking on him; he endured it for another moment, and then, exclaiming " It is my father," he crossed himself, and waited with awe and sickness to hear a voice address him; but no, all was still, silent as the grave; the silence made it too horrible to bear, and bursting out " I cannot endure this," Albert, with almost superhuman exertion, dashed into the room, and reaching the window shutters, the position and mode of fastening of which he knew from those in the next room: he unfastened them, threw them open, and let in a burst of light which, in an instant, exhibited everything to his view which, a moment before, was hidden; the effect was like that of enchantment upon him, although springing from so simple a cause, and overcome by the violence of his feelings, he sunk down almost in a swoon upon a chair, with his face covered by his hands. He was naturally very brave, possessing high moral courage, and a great amount of coolness and decision; but as this was not a case of ordinary danger, they were not called into play, his feelings, his spirits, his superstition (every one possesses the last more or less) were affected by preceding events, and rendered him weaker than he would have been if he had not previously been prepared for something supernatural; in a little time he recovered himself and looked around him; he breathed more freely as no object but the furniture and decorations of the room met his enquiring gaze; he walked round the room, and almost smiled, while a blush mounted to his brow when he found it was his father's portrait, painted in oil, the size of life, which had so strongly affected him upon his entrance; he gazed upon it, it was well executed, and there was some feeling of pride passed through Albert's mind as he looked on the large blue eyes, the well formed features, and the manly expression which played over them; he was habited in the costume of the period, and on a small gold slab placed in the centre of the base of the gold frame which surrounded the portrait, was written in High Dutch—

PHILIP VANDERDECKEN,
Captain of the Good Ship
AMSTELREDAMME.
1620.

Albert defending Winken Kroots' house.

Albert read the inscription, looked on the picture, and turned sadly away; upon the opposite side of the room was another portrait, it was of a lady, painted by the same hand; she was young, and exquisitely beautiful; there was an expression of happiness upon the features, pleasant to behold, and Albert wondered who it could be—so young, so beautiful.

"Good God! my mother!" he exclaimed as he saw an inscription on the frame which was of similar make to that which held his father's portrait.

ESTELLE VANDEDECKEN,
Wife of
Captain Vanderdecken,
1620.

"Can grief," he apostrophized, "make so awful a change in the human countenance as thine exhibited, dear sainted mother? I can now see too terribly what you have borne—suffered, since that fearful night; may thy spirit realize all the bliss Heaven bestows!"

Albert again proceeded, after breathing a long sigh, to scrutinize the apartment; there was a table in the room with a quantity of things strewn upon it; he knew, he felt, the object of his search lay upon that table; he was conscious his search was to end there, and with an intense desire

No. 4.

to know his fate, he still kept from it with that strange contrariety or feeling which the human character exhibits when an evil is hanging over it; there is an enormous desire to grapple with it and know the worst, yet it is put off until it can be put off no longer, bringing with it a regret that it was not met before: if that table had been a magnet, and Albert a body which had an affinity for it, he could not have been more strongly drawn to it, yet he would not go to it, although it occupied all his thoughts; he proceeded. By the side of the fire-place, in a niche, stood a handsome cabinet with glass doors, in the inside of which were curtains, which had been a red silk, but had now faded to an orange yellow; a bunch of keys were hanging to one which fitted the lock, and Albert turned it, and found a large quantity of silver vessels for domestic use, china, glass, and various other things in the way of ornaments and curiosities, brought, as he supposed, by his father, from the east. When he had satisfied himself with looking at the contents of the cabinet he drew the key from the lock, and took the bunch in his hand; underneath the cabinet—indeed, forming part of it, were folding doors, and these he opened: some Indian bows, large shells, the skull of a porpoise, and many other things, met his eyes, and among them a box of about two feet square; it was of oak, clasped and belted with steel; he laid hold or it to draw it out, and found it required a very great deal of strength to do it; when he got it out he wondered what it could contain that made it so heavy; he kneeled down to open it, but was some time ere he found a key to fit it; at last he succeeded, and opened it; it was full of small bags, he took up one and unfastened it; it was full of guilders; he took up another, it was similar; a third, a fourth; they were all full or guilders! there must have been at least eighteen or twenty thousand in that box; and, from great poverty, Albert suddenly found himself the possessor of great wealth. He was bewildered, he knew the straits to which his mother had been reduced from want of money many times, and yet there was a very large sum of money—a fortune—in her possession; he could not account for it but by his mother's excessive horror at any thoughts of entering the room. "She did not even see the packet," he ejaculated.

"THE PACKET!" uttered the voice he had heard before. He leaped to his feet with the bound of an antelope, and turned his eyes in every direction, but in vain, no form, spectre or human, met his gaze.

"It shall be so," he exclaimed aloud; "if the packet is there," cried he, as he approached the table, "I will read it."

"READ IT!" echoed the voice.

Albert shuddered. "Is this real, Holy Virgin?" he exclaimed, energetically, crossing himself; and, drawing the relic from his bosom, he kissed it with great devotion; "or is it but a strange echo I have heard? it is awfully mysterious." He paused for a moment, then drew a breath, and walked firmly to the table; there was a quantity of things lying upon it—books, muslin; he could not see the packet, but he knew where it was; he felt a horrid surprise that he, who had never been in that room since the packet had been placed there—and at that time a young child of three years' old, had never any idea where it had been, or even that it had been placed there, until the last few days—should know the exact spot it occupied.

"God of Heaven! it must be real," he exclaimed, as he lifted up the book, and *there lay the packet!*

Albert turned sick and faint when he saw it; here was fearful evidence that his mother had spoken *truth*—had not been deceived by an illusion, and that the voice he had so recently heard was also no fabrication of the brain. What could the packet contain? his mother had said, a means of alleviating the duration of his father's punishment; "It must be so," he cried, "and I am to be the instrument through which it will be accomplished." He stretched forth his hand and took up the letter: had he taken a piece of ice in his fingers it would have chilled the blood in them less than did that letter; he thrilled as the superscription caught his eye; it bore his name—was addressed to himself; he looked again, and rubbed his eyes; he was not mistaken; it was directed to "Albert Vanderdecken." In a state of desperation he tore open the seal, and read—

"ALBERT,

"My son, my awful doom has been revealed to you, and its cause; that I was not ever vile, the permission to make known a means by which my terrible judgment may be superseded, will prove; it is only my conduct at that one period of my existence, which brought down the fearful anger of the Almighty upon me, that you have caused to blush for my memory: let that pass.

"You wear about your person a relic of the Holy Cross—it was worn by your mother, and given by me to her; I received it from my family, to which it has descended through successive generations, from an ancestor who walked in the presence of our Lord of Jerusalem.

"That relic is the means by which my soul is to be saved from eternal judgment.

"I must receive it upon the deck of the vessel in which I made that awful oath; by bowing myself humbly and contritely before it, kiss it with the humility and reverence arising from pure and sincere repentance, my doom will pass away, and my spirit will find repose.

"Albert, with you rests the accomplishment of this; if you die without fulfilling it, the means pass away with you—for they are limited—and I shall carry out my dreadful doom, of BEATING ABOUT UNTIL THE DAY OF JUDGMENT.—Farewell! Albert.

"PHILIP VANDERDECKEN."

"I am to accomplish my father's salvation," said Albert, when he had finished the letter, the perusal of which he had gone through with breathless interest, until every word was impressed vividly upon his memory; "this, then, is to be my destiny."

"THE DESTINY," again exclaimed the hollow voice, and a loud crash ensued, as if of some heavy body falling. Albert looked round in an instant, and saw his father's picture had fallen from the wall upon the ground; he turned to the letter, which he imagined he held in his hand, and it was GONE! no trace of it to be seen.

"Mysterious Providence!" he exclaimed, "this is too much for my brain to bear;" and, pressing his hands to his burning temples, he fell insensible upon the floor.

CHAPTER IV.

AN ATTEMPTED ROBBERY.—BLOODSHED.—RESCUE.

THE sun was sinking in the west when Albert came to his senses; the long shadows which the sinking luminary cast, and the subdued light, gave a sombre hue to the apartment in which Albert still remained—he endeavoured to collect his scattered thoughts; was all he had undergone real, or was it a terrible dream? Alas! it was no dream, he was in the fatal apartment, and his father's picture still lay upon the floor; he dreaded to look round him, as though he should meet the cold, icy glare of some spectre; the room seemed too close for him to breathe, it was like a furnace; his breast heaved, and with an oppression almost to death; he rushed wildly from the apartment, he sought the fields, he walked on and on; the cool air relieved him, and he breathed more freely; he came to a copse shaded with trees, he threw himself down, and reflected on his situation, upon what his future course must be; there was but one line marked out for him to pursue, and that he determined to follow, come what may. It was probable that his future life would be a series of trials and vicissitudes; but whose is not in this world of disappointment? they occur, in a greater or less degree, to different persons, but the average is made by the amount of fortitude with which the mind of those bearing the greatest evils are invested—enabling them to bear misfortunes of greater magnitude with the same equanimity which those whose trials are less great possess. Albert consoled himself with the reflection that he was alone in the world, and therefore had no tie which could cause him regret at devoting his life and happiness to the accomplishment of so extraordinary a task as the averting of his father's doom: this might appear a selfish feeling, but Albert did not possess any selfishness in his character, and the feeling was rather that there would be no one who could suffer by his spending his life in his devotion to his duty, than one of regret that there would be little happiness in store for him. His dear mother had been the only tie he possessed, and she had passed away; what should prevent him immediately seeking some method of commencing his task? he had wealth; nothing to detain him at Amsterdam; and therefore he resolved to go on board some ship bound for the East Indies, and see what fate had in store for him. As he lay still reflecting, he felt some surprise that the beautiful Aylmine was mixed up with all his reflections; he found his thoughts constantly recurring to her in spite of himself, and he had an unconscious pleasure in dwelling on the loveliness of her form, and also upon the power he possessed of paying Mynheer Winken Kroots his due—he could keep his word, and she would see that he did; he thought he would go the first thing in the morning, " but, perhaps," he thought again, " I shall not see her, the little wretch Winken will keep her from my sight—what an extraordinary little beast it is !—he never can be her father —absurd, impossible—I will see her, I'll make him let me—" and then he sighed. " But why should I ?" he asked himself, mournfully, " why should I ? I that have to devote my days to the fulfilment of a duty which I will endeavour to do, religiously and scrupulously; so, prosper my hopes of eternal happiness hereafter;" and, devoutly crossing himself, he kissed the sacred relic fervently. "Yes," he continued, "why should I tempt my fate by again seeing her—she is nothing to me now, I cannot be aught to her; it will be better that I should not go; I will send Winken Kroots his guilders, and leave Amsterdam, if fate wills it so, for ever." These thoughts had hardly passed through his mind when footsteps broke upon his ear; he listened, and distinguished voices; they stopped very close to him, but the trees concealed him from their view.

"I tell you" cried one, "that he has got plenty of shiners; I am sure of it."

"Yes," retorted a second, "but how do you know?"

"Why, I'll tell you," returned the first, "I was very ill once, and he attended me; every one said I was on my way to the other world?"

"What, below!" laughed the third person.

"No matter whether above or below," gruffly returned the first speaker, "I was dying, so they said, and Winken Kroots put me to rights again; before I was quite recovered I used to crawl to his house for advice and medicine, because he charged me less, and I gave him all his bottles back—he used to be very particular about that; and once when I went I found the door ajar, I pushed it open, and nobody was there; I entered quietly, and stole up stairs; and what do you think I saw?" he inquired of his two companions, with a perfect assurance that they could not guess.

"Don't know," returned the second speaker.

"Can't tell," exclaimed the third.

"Why," returned the first, "of course you could'nt; how should you? I was uncommonly surprised myself, I rubbed my eyes, and stared as if they'd have come out of my head; I'm sure they must have been as large as two silver watches," he speculated. Now, at that day, watches were about the size of dessert plates, and it may reasonably be concluded, if he spoke truth, that he was very much surprised.

"Well! well! go on;" impatiently cried the third speaker.

"Don't hurry me," replied the story steller, "I'm coming to it as fast as I can, aint I? Well, there I saw Winken Kroots kneeling at a chest loaded with money bags, and a girl standing by his side, the beautifullest, loveliest angel I ever clapped my eyes on. Lord, ha' mercy, I cried, what a darling; as I said this, Winken shut down his chest with a loud bang, jumped up, and asked me who I was, what I wanted, and how I came there? I asked him if he did'nt know me? and then he said, oh yes, and tried to laugh, but it was'nt a bit like a laugh; he called me his very good friend, and said he was looking out some medicines, that was all—that was all; I nodded my head, but I knew better; I looked for the girl, but she had vanished; I never saw her go, or even heard her; I asked about her, who and what she was? he told me she was his daughter; well, I went away with my medicine, and soon got well, although I said I was not, and used to go very often to try and see her, but I could'nt, the old rat kept her too close; I could'nt get her out of my head—I tried, but it was no use; at last I proposed to marry her."

Albert opened his eyes and strained his sense of hearing to catch every word.

"I offered her my hand; the old dog actually jeered at me, and refused me; I raved, stamped, swore, pleaded, persuaded, threatened, it was all of no use, he refused me, and I swore to be revenged, and I will;—D—n me, I'll tear the little skinny reptile into shreds, and carry off his daughter, I will!"

"Will you?" thought Albert; "not if I can help it!"

"Well, Eyloff Brabant," returned the second speaker, "your information is pretty good, and we will act upon it; we will share the money and the girl between us."

"No!" almost shouted Eyloff Brabant, "the girl is mine, I shall have her to myself; that I've made up my mind to."

"Take care you are not disappointed," thought Albert.

"I am willing to make an allowance for her," continued Eyloff, "in my share of the money; but the girl shall be mine if it costs me my life."

"Oh, you may have her in welcome, if you give up a share of money for her; what say you, Paul?" said the third speaker, addressing the second.

"With all my heart," was the reply; "but how much money may we expect to get?"

"About five thousand guilders, as near as I can judge," replied Eyloff; "if we get that I will take the girl and a thousand guilders, and you shall divide the four thousand between you."

"Very fair," exclaimed Paul; "but suppose there is not so much."

"Well, I will take less in proportion," replied Brabant.

"Agreed!" cried the other two.

"And now," said Brabant, "we will wait until the moon is up, and then we can get to the house, and, most likely, Winken Kroots will be at home; we can draw him out on some pretence or other, then dispatch him, and the rest of our work will be easy."

"Then I have no time to lose," thought Albert, "now. I hope my wind and legs will befriend me." He stole gently and silently from the copse; the sun was already touching the hill, and in the opposite heaven the moon was beginning to shed its influence over the earth. Albert knew his ground well, but was compelled to go rather a roundabout way to avoid detection; he started off, and his speed did honour to his will; a very short time elapsed, and he was at the door of Winken Kroots, knocking as loudly as he did on his first visit, but not with such an errand, although life and death were concerned in his mission; he waited a little while, but no answer was returned, he knocked again several times, loudly and rapidly; he waited, still he had no reply; he then began to batter at the door with all his strength, and shout for Winken Kroots, but no Winken Kroots came; the time was getting on, and there was every prospect of the three men arriving before he could effect an entrance; the very thought spurred him on.

"Winken Kroots, there are thieves about to attack your house; let me in—I have come to save you; it is I, Albert Vanderdecken; be speedy, or you will be too late. Open, open!"

But still no answer was returned, and anger began to take the place of an endeavour to serve. "Does the miserly little vagabond expect I am going to steal his money myself, or his daughter—Ah, Aylmine! she must be saved whatever befals the rest, be it Winken Kroots or even his money." Again he hammered at the door, but with no better success. "Can Winken be out? it must be so, and yet it is scarcely likely at this hour," thought he; "however, I'll not give it up yet. Ah," he exclaimed, as an idea struck him, "I'll bring him out if he is at home. Winken Kroots, Winken, I have come to pay you the four guilders, the amount of your bill; open the door, it is I, Albert Vanderdecken." He put his ear to the door, but heard no approaching footsteps, and was about to give a dash at the door with his foot in an excess of passion, when the casement above him opened, and a voice demanded the cause of this clatter; Albert, ere he raised his head, knew it was Aylmine that accosted him, and, with a feeling approaching to delight, jumped from the door, and exclaimed, with earnestness and rapidity,

"Maiden, open the door, lose not a moment, I entreat you. I have just overheard a plan to rob your house, murder your father, and carry off you."

"A rare collection of vile intentions," uttered the maiden.

"It is true, I assure you," eagerly said Albert.

"How am I to know it?" demanded Aylmine.

"You know little of me, maiden, if you suppose I would be guilty of a lie—one too of such magnitude as this would be, if what I tell you were false—you wrong me!" exclaimed Albert, proudly, while the blood suffused his cheeks.

"I know but little of you," retorted Aylmine, "merely what took place in a scene of violence; how then, from that circumstance—an attempt to destroy my father—am I to take what you tell me upon trust? how know I you speak the truth?"

"By my honour, with which I would scorn to part, while I had a breath of life in my lungs; and by my word, which I will pledge to you, and which I have never, since I knew what truth meant, broken, so help me Heaven!" cried Albert, with flushed cheeks and a swelling chest. Aylmine gazed upon him, and believed that she read sincerity plainly impressed upon his brow.

"I will trust you," she said, "I heard my father say you always kept your word; you cannot mean me wrong."

"I do not, as I hope to rest in peace when I have quitted this dreary world," uttered Albert, fervently; "believe me, maiden, it is only thy safety that has brought me hither, I fear I should not have exhibited all this patience else: but, haste thee, maiden, the sun has already sunk behind the western hill, and when the moon is up, which will shortly be, they will be here," urgently concluded he. The casement closed, and Albert waited for a few moments, and then he heard the door unbar; in another moment he was inside, and, closing the door, hastily fastened it. Aylmine shrunk back, and faintly exclaimed,

"You have passed your word, Mynheer Vanderdecken, that"—

"My action was hasty," replied Albert, interrupting her, "and may have startled you, but I know there is not a moment to lose, and I acted upon an impulse; I meant not to alarm you, and as to harming you—" and he gazed fervently upon her, "it is not in human nature to do so."

"And yet," said the maiden, still keeping back, with her eyes upon the ground, " you tell me there is an attempt to be made to carry me off within a short time."

" I overheard it," said Albert; " but surely you would not call a rasc like the scoundrel who purposed committing so much villany, a portion of human nature ?"

" Are you sure they meant my father's house was the one they intended to plunder ?" asked Aylmine.

" They mentioned his name," returned Albert, " and the fellow who proposed to bear you off was called by one of his companions, Eyloff Brabant ; he professed himself violently in love with you, and said he had made an offer of marriage, but had been scornfully rejected ; for this he vowed revenge against your father, and that he would carry you off."

" There was a man of that name who, I believe, did make some such offer, but he was such a horrid-looking creature that I shuddered when I saw him, which once I did, but it was but for a moment."

" So I heard him say," answered Albert; " and now, lady, if you have any fire-arms, let me have them, and I care not how soon they come."

" There is a brace of pistols and a carbine in the surgery, which my father always keeps loaded, and I can also show you where there is plenty of ammunition. Follow me," said Aylmine, and led the way to the room in which the reader was first introduced to Winken Kroots compounding drugs. Aylmine pointed out the arms, and Albert took them. " These," he said, will be of good service ; but where is your father ? I concluded he was out by not seeing him, and have not thought to inquire for him until this moment."

" He was suddenly called to attend a patient," returned Aylmine, " but I expect him home soon."

" I pray heaven," ejaculated Albert, " he may not return too soon, and be met by those ruffians ; they will surely kill him if he falls in with them."

" I fervently hope not," uttered Aylmine, in an agitated tone.

" Ha !" exclaimed Albert, as he saw Aylmine return a dagger to her girdle. " Was not that dagger destined for my breast had I deceived you ?"

" No !" said Aylmine, as she dropped her head, while the colour mounted to her brow ; " it was intended for my own, had necessity required it ; I prefer death to disgrace."

" Noble girl," cried Albert, in a fit of enthusiasm, and gazed with an ardent unconcealed admiration upon her beautiful face ; Aylmine looked up and their eyes met ; there was more spoken, and understood between them by that glance than ordinary circumstances could have done in six months ; they both felt confused, and they were spared further embarrassment by a loud knock at the door, and the voice of Eyloff Brabant exclaiming,

" Winken Kroots, open the door, I want you to attend a friend of mine who lies dangerously ill a short distance from here."

" It is them," cried Albert, " we must to the room above, and attack them from that point."

" Winken Kroots," roared the voice outside the door.

Sudden appearance of the Phantom Ship.

Aylmine ran lightly up the stairs, followed by Albert, and entered the room; he gently opened the casement, having first taken the precaution to bring no light with him;—he looked out and beckoned Aylmine to him, she came and looked out—there stood three men in the bright moonlight watching the door earnestly, ready to pounce upon whoever appeared at the door, they seemed like terriers on the watch for rats; they grew impatient.

"Winken Kroots, Winken Kroots;" roared Eyloff, "you know me, it is Eyloff Brabant that calls;—a friend a very particular dear friend, lies at the point of death."

"Say your mother," suggested Paul.

"Winken Kroots," shouted Eyloff, "it is my mother, who is dying. Why don't you come? perhaps she will be dead before you can get there if you don't make haste. I will pay you well—answer me—come; if you don't come directly I'll break your door down, and beat you to a jelly, I will, you shrivelled, skinny, wretched rat, so beware; open the door, or I'll beat it in."

Still there was no answer, and Albert smiled, though mournfully, when he recollected how passionately, and how similarly he had halloed to Winken when he had come to fetch him to attend his poor mother; he

No. 5.   F started as he felt a light hand press his shoulder, and turning saw the sweet eyes of Aylmine beaming on him kindly as she said—

"Albert, you have spoken truth—forgive me, for I wronged you."

"I honour your prudence, in acting as you did," replied Albert, "and, therefore, there is nothing for me to forgive : but prithee retire, the rogues are after something by their silence, and I may be, perhaps, called into action in a manner which may bring danger upon you if you are near me, leave me; there are only three, and I am sure I can manage them."

"Excuse me," replied Aylmine, "if there is danger, and you in it, it is on my account; I cannot suffer you to share it alone; I can reload your weapons when they are discharged."

"You?" exclaimed Albert, in a tone of surprise.

"Yes," returned the maiden, "some years since I was accustomed to it, and the time may come when I can relate a portion of my early life to you, which will prove the truth of my assertion."

"I care not how soon so great a pleasure may come, although I cannot doubt your word, Aylmine, even though I tried; but hist, this is the cause of their silence," said Albert, as he directed Aylmine's attention to the conduct of the robbers. They were busily employed in carrying faggots from a small outhouse contiguous, and placing them at the door; when they had made a good sized heaps Eyloff exclaimed :

"Winken Kroots, will you open the door ? if you do not at once I am prepared to do it for you in a manner that will astonish you most disagreeably."

Still they received no answer, and Paul struck a light with a flint and steel, which he carried with him to light his pipe, and prepared to set fire to the faggots, and then burn the door, probably the house down; just as he stooped down to light the bundle, he received a bullet through his brain, from a pistol fired by Albert, and fell dead upon the ground; his companions were horribly startled by the report, and more by the sight of the dead body of their friend. It, however, inflamed their rage, and they were not long in discovering from what quarter the shot had proceeded : a bullet whizzing past the head of Albert, told him they were acquainted with his lurking place; he heard a shout, he knew it was the voice of Winken Kroots, he saw the little man come bounding and jumping along, and Eyloff Brabant prepare to meet him; he took an aim at the scoundrel Brabant, but he was in so direct a line with Winken Kroots that he had a very strong fear if he missed Eyloff, he should hit Winken, a sort of shooting at a pigeon and killing a crow he wished to avoid; to make sure of his mark he turned his aim to the third man, who had twice fired at him, and both times missed him; Albert took a better aim than he did, for he shot him through the heart; the man leaped up in agony, and then fell down a corpse. There was now no time to lose if Winken's life was to be saved, and Albert crying to Aylmine :

"Aylmine, show me how to unfasten the door, and let me out as speedily as possible, or I fear unless I can reach the spot immediately your father's life will be sacrificed."

Aylmine did not talk, she acted, and Albert passed through the door ere he could have imagined it possible to have withdrawn the fastenings;

he had not to hesitate in which direction to turn, the voice of Winken was high in the air, and his body, Albert saw, was low on the ground, struggling madly and desperately with Eyloff Brabant. Albert sprung up to the spot to assist the fallen doctor; as he reached him he was startled by a shriek, and Eyloff Brabant flung his arms wildly in the air, and the next instant pressing them convulsively to his side, staggered away for a short distance, and then with a heavy groan fell down on the earth lifeless. Albert stood motionless with surprise for a few seconds, but he had scarcely time to reflect ere Winken was up, and darting past him, rushed into the house; he followed the little man, who was met at the door by Aylmine, and heard him exclaim :

"You are safe!—the robbers—yes—have they got my money? the monsters, the thieves—all my little earnings and scrapings—the cheat, the cut-throats."

"I am safe, Father, thank heaven and this gentleman, and your money is also untouched," said Aylmine.

"This gentleman," echoed Winken turning round like a cat that expects her meat to be taken from her, and stands with a claw ready for the purloiner, "who is this gentleman?"

"He has preserved me from an infamy worse ten fold than the loss of life," returned Aylmine, "and saved the house from being fired, your money from being stolen, and killed two of the ruffians."

"Sir, I am very much indebted to you," returned Winken, "my money is very little—I am very poor, if I lose it I should be completely ruined; you are very good—good night, sir," he concluded, as though he would feel satisfied by the departure of Albert.

"You do not appear to recollect me; I am Albert Vanderdecken," said our hero.

Winken started as though some sharp instrument had been inserted in some tender part of his person. "Albet Vanderrkecken?" echoed he in a tone beween alarm and doubt.

"Yes, Winken Kroot," retorted Albert, "the same person from whom you stole the relic; and who is indebted to you four guilders which you can have in the morning were they twice four thousand."

"Twice four thousand?" reiterated Winken with amazement depicted in his countenance.

"Yes," returned Albert, "I have above three times that sum to meet your demand, were it necessary."

"Twice four thousand; three times that sum—twenty-four thousand guilders !" muttered the miserly remnant of a physician, "why then it's of no consequence to you to pay me."

"None," replied Albert, "why?" he questioned.

"Because, although I am poor, indeed wretchedly poor, I would have consented to have forgiven you the debt, for saving my little property to night," said Kroots, eking the words out as if he was half afraid Albert would accept his offer, "but as you are so rich you do not mind paying me."

"Father!" said Aylmine, with a look of shame at his paltriness of feeling.

"I shall most certainly pay you," said Albert, as a smile chased away the scornful curl of his upper lip, "I promised you, you know, and I always keep my word," he concluded, half imitating the manner in which Winken Kroots had addressed him at their last meeting.

" That will do, that will do;" cried Winken in a delighted tone.

" Now let me beg of you," said Albert turning to Aylmine, " to retire to rest; I will watch for the remainder of the night, and will take care that you be not further alarmed."

" Nay," observed Aylmine, " there is no need for watching, I am sure we shall not be disturbed by marauders again to-night; and I am convinced after the excitement you require repose, therefore do you, Albert, seek your bed, and may your slumbers be as light and free as I can wish them."

Albert smiled, and shook his head mournfully, as though he doubted the possibility of such an occurrence, but he said :

" Aylmine, pray let me act as I have requested, for though I may not be suffered by you to remain here, yet I should stay till morning near the house ; for I could not be easy while I thought there was a possibility of harm approaching you."

" Be it as you will, Albert," returned Aylmine, your kindness is very great, and I thank you heartily and sincerely for the services which this night you have rendered us."

" Name them not, Aylmine, 'tis but a poor return for the fright I occasioned you a short time since;" replied Albert, and now good night, may the Holy Mother have you in her keeping."

" Farewell !" said Aylmine, and extending her hand to him; he took it, and acting on the impulse of the moment carried it to his lips; he had barely imprinted a kiss upon them when he reflected upon the act, and turned his eyes upon Aylmine to see if she was offended, and beheld her gazing upon him with a look which seemed as if it would read his inmost thoughts: he returned her gaze with an open, sincere look which seemed to say frankly, ' I have no foul thought, my heart is clear from stain.' Aylmine seemed satisfied with her scrutiny, and her eyes fell; she did not withdraw her hand, and Albert fancied he felt a slight pressure on his; it was but slight, but something told him that it was intended, and with a gratified feeling he left the room, and seeking the street-door, walked up and down in front of the house until the morning sun came glancing over the hills.

CHAP. V.

A STORY, A REMOVAL, AND A MARRIAGE.

AYLMINE came down early in the morning, and found Albert leaning against the door-post, she found he was not aware of her presence, and she laid her hand lightly on his shoulder; he started hastily round with an extraordinary expression, not exactly of fear, but betokening apprehensions of something awful; when he saw that it was Aylmine, the expression passed away, as a cloud from before the face of the sun, and he smiled as he looked on her beautiful face with the same expression he had shown when he parted from her—if a crimson flush which ran rapidly over his features be excepted; Aylmine witnessed the remarkable change with some surprise, but would not appear to notice it, and affecting a gaiety of tone, which she did not exactly feel, she said:

"What, sleeping upon your post? a drowsy sentinel makes a bad soldier, Mynheer Vanderdecken."

"No, indeed, Aylmine, I was not sleeping, I was deeply abstracted by some thoughts which have a very deep influence over me, or I should have been aware of your approach ere I had seen you," returned Albert with feeling.

"Before you had seen me, impossible!" exclaimed Aylmine, "your prescience must be great indeed to tell that; how would you accomplish it?"

"I should feel it on my heart," replied Albert, earnestly.

Aylmine remained silent for a few moments, and Albert spoke not; at length the maiden broke it by requesting him to enter the house and partake of some refreshment, to which he acquiesced in silence, and met Winken at the breakfast table. The little doctor was exceedingly gracious, the understanding of Albert's wealth had produced it with much greater force than any feeling of gratitude for the safety of his property and even his life, which would have been assuredly forfeited but for the timely interposition of Albert; they discoursed upon the last night's occurrences, and upon the necessity of acquainting the proper authorities of what had taken place. This, after the breakfast was over, Winken Kroots took upon himself to do, and Albert was left alone with Aylmine; they sat for a few minutes in silence, when Albert said:

"Aylmine, I am about to ask you a question, it is a strange one, I own, and you may deem it impertinent; it may appear so, but I do not mean it as such, believe me; and if you have the least objection to answer it, I beg of you to say so, and I will not again offend your ears with the request," he paused for a moment, and Aylmine wondering what it could possibly be, observed:

"If Mynheer Vanderdecken will state his question, I will return an answer if in my power; I think I know too much of him to fear that my ears should be offended by any question or remark he might make."

"Aylmine, you do me justice, I could not at least to you, and I think not to any one;" returned Albert with fervour, "I thank you for your remark and now let me ask you to call me in future Albert, you will be doing me a kindness in consenting."

"Is that all?" said Aylmine quickly, and then checked herself, "I—I meant," she hesitated, and then continued frankly, "if you wish it, certainly."

"Many thanks," returned Albert, "but that was not the question that I prefaced by begging you not to answer unless it met with your perfect concurrence to do so, it is this: I cannot believe after looking at you, and knowing your mind by your actions, that you can be the daughter of Winken Kroots; so utterly opposite in person and mind are you to him that I cannot credit that you are his child."

Aylmine smiled as Albert concluded, and said, "Your conjecture is correct, I am not his daughter, and if you do not mind my wearying you by a little history of who I am, I will tell you."

"Aylmine!" ejaculated Albert, as though he wondered how it was possible such a thing as being wearied by anything she could say or do, could ever have crossed her imagination.

Aylmine laughed, and commenced her history, "My mother," was the daughter of a Bey at Cairo, [she was beloved and loved a young man of inferior birth to herself, and to whom, therefore, there was little prospect of being united with the consent of her father; but they loved each other too tenderly, too dearly to bear the idea of a separation, and they determined to hazard everything in a secret marriage, and endeavour to escape to Europe. Winken Kroots, who is a native of Holland, was practising as a *hakim*, or physician, having embraced the Mahometan faith, and it became known to my mother's father, that he had amassed considerable wealth, and he determined to seek some pretence or other to seize it. My mother mentioned this to her husband, and advised him to inform Winken Kroots of this circumstance, and to offer if he would assist them to escape to enable him by timely information to carry off his wealth; her husband, my father, approved of the scheme, and proposed it to Winken Kroot's, who readily concurred in any plan which offered a prospect of saving his money, and when they had laid their plans, they proceeded with beating hearts to execute them. They succeeded in making their escape, my father, mother, Winken Kroots, and his money; but in crossing the Great Desert the caravan with which they travelled was attacked by Bedouin Arabs, many of the party slain and the remainder were taken prisoners, among whom was my mother, father, Winken Kroots, and his money. For a period of three years my father and mother remained with the Arabs, as did also Winken Kroots, whose life they spared in consideration of his abilities as a physician; I was born, and was some solace to my mother in her captivity which lasted six years; after my birth, my father, whom the Arabs had forced to join in all their plundering excursions, was shot dead, and my mother survived but a short time. Thus was I left an orphan among a wandering tribe of robbers; Winken Kroots had been sent for by my mother while in the arms of death, and she placed me in his care; I believe that there was some very forcible motive which induced him to consent and act as he has done to me, for his inordinate passion for money assures me that but for some powerful incentive he would long since have left me in the world alone and friendless. After my mother's death four years passed away, and I was still with the Arabs, mixing in scenes of sudden strife, bloodshed, rapid changes, from place to place, now in want now in plenty; this life did not suit Winken Kroots, he could not amass money, and, therefore, he left no means untried to effect his escape. One day an attack was made upon a caravan of merchants crossing the Desert, but it proved too strong for the Arabs, they were beaten off to their very tents. Winken Kroots made himself known to the chief of the victors, and begged of them to take him, myself, and his goods with them; they consented, and I have every reason to believe that he was not very particular in taking only his own. We went to Damascus, and there Winken made a vast sum. The Cadi cast an avaricious eye upon it, and a favourite of his dying while under the charge of Winken Kroots, was taken by the Cadi as a pretext for taking the whole of his wealth, and he barely escaped with his life; he took me with him, and we got to Grenada; after he had made again a very large sum there, for he was very expeditious in getting a heap of money together; we quitted Grenada for Amsterdam, but coming home we encountered the Flying Dutchman——good heavens, Albert, what is the matter?" cried Aylmine interrupting herself as Albert started back as though he had been shot.

"It is nothing—a pang through my heart—my head—it is gone," said Albert with confusion; "pray proceed," he continued with intense eagerness—she had mentioned his father's ship, and it had set his brain in a whirl. Aylmine was not exactly satisfied with his answer, but as she could not understand the reason of his sudden shock, she proceeded:

"We encountered the Phantom Ship, which I am given to understand is fatal to every vessel which falls in with it, and it is to beat about until the day of judgment with all the crew, in consequence of the blasphemy of the Captain."

"I know, I know;" groaned Albert, "pray go on!"

"You are ill Albert; what is it?" asked Aylmine with interest; "I am sure I have unconsciously said something which has thus affected you."

"Nay 'tis nothing;" replied Albert affecting a smile, but without success, "I am waiting anxiously for the remainder of your story."

Aylmine shook her head doubtfully, and proceeded, while every word she uttered respecting the spectre ship was impressed with intense force on Albert's heart.

"It was about seven in the evening," she said, "the wind had been down all day scarce a breath stirred, but as evening approached indications were given of a coming storm, and the sailors were prepared to meet it. It soon came with great violence from the point we were leaving, and blew us forward at a tremendous rate; we saw a heavy mist rising, and as I said before, it was about seven in the evening when the man at the mast head cried out, 'sail ahead,' we looked and there appeared to be a vessel coming towards us furiously, with every sail set, coming also completely against the wind: as it came near us some one shrieked that it would run us down; on it came nearer and nearer, the sailors hailed it, shouted, screamed to them to turn their ship, but in vain, and it seemed to come quite on our ship and *sail over it*, without doing us the slightest damage. We turned and looked in the direction it had taken, saw no vestige of it remaining; it was then that a sailor cried out it was the Flying Dutchman; I inquired the meaning, and was told the legend I mentioned to you; after the vision had taken place the storm raged more furiously than ever. The ship sprung a leak, and was rapidly sinking; everything moveable was thrown overboard to lighten her, Winken Kroots' chest of money among the different articles, and they had a difficulty to prevent him jumping after it. The leak gained so fast on the pumps that they found it impossible to keep the vessel above water; they therefore took to the boats, and abandoned it. For three long weary days we were tossed upon the sea in a wretched boat, and were at the end of that time picked up by a vessel bound for Amsterdam. They treated us with every kindness, and we arrived here safely where we have remained ever since, and so ends my history."

"Many thanks, Aylmine," said Albert, who had listened with fearful attention to that portion of it which related to his father. "I have learned something which I never dreamed of hearing, which I feel an obligation upon me to say as an apology for my strange conduct."

"I was convinced of it, Albert," returned Aylmine, "and believe me I am not going to speak from an inquisitive feeling; but I have heard my father—I mean Winken Kroots—I have called him father from a child, and cannot forget it now."

"I was sure he was not your father," said Albert, with enthusiasm.

Aylmine smiled as she continued. "I have heard Winken Kroots speak of your mother's poverty; of a mysterious chamber in your house being closed for many years; and I witnessed your extraordinary desire to recover the relic which Winken Kroots so very unceremoniously took; also your sudden accession to wealth; have they not some relation to your abstraction this morning, and to something which I have mentioned in the course of my history? and the depression on your spirits arises from the same cause, does it not?

"I feel that you are paying me an affectionate compliment, Aylmine," said Albert, "in taking an interest in anything relating to me, and I feel bound to tell you that there is a mystery hangs over me; and your conjectures are correct respecting those things which are connected with it; more I do not feel at liberty to disclose, or I would unburthen my heart to you."

"You do me an honour and a kindness in saying so Albert," replied Aylmine, "I seek not to know more than you may desire to tell, and so let us change the conversation."

"I wish you," said Albert, "to give your consent to something I thought of while watching this morning, which I wish to see accomplished most earnestly; which is, that the report of Winken Kroots being a rich miser is gaining ground every day; there are a great many unprincipled villains abroad, as you may judge by last night's events. When they discover Winken's wealth no stone will be left unturned until they obtain it, perhaps at the expense of life. This house situated in a lonely spot, easy of attack, and with only an old weak man and a delicate female to defend it, is not so easy to preserve. I have therefore concluded that you can with your father come to Floris Grant to my house, and live in it; you will both be safer there, and I shall have no need of the house while I am at sea."

"At sea?" echoed Aylmine with surprise.

"Yes, Aylmine," said Albert, "I am going to the Indies."

"May I inquire for what reason?" asked the maiden, who had turned pale when she had first heard his intention, and was now red with a blush mantling her cheeks. "You spoke of riches, there can be no necessity for you to go."

"There is a terrible necessity," returned Albert mournfully, which wealth cannot effect; it is a duty which I have sworn to fulfil, and I must keep my oath. It is my destiny!" As he said the last words he started violently and looked over his shoulder, shuddered, and then gazed round the room; he had heard the hollow voice repeat "THY DESTINY." Aylmine who had noticed the act had followed the direction of his eyes with rapidity, but saw nothing—heard nothing; she turned anxiously to him,

" He raised her hand to his lips, and imprinted a kiss upon it."

and saw him with his face buried in his hands. She approached him and leaning tenderly over him, inquired the cause of his emotion. He drew his hands from his face and looked up, as he said—

" Aylmine, there is an extraordinary mystery connected with me, which affects, and will affect my future life. I do not feel at present that I ought or can mention it, but a time may perhaps come when I will tell you all ; if I tell it to mortal it shall be to thee ; but let it pass. Will you promise me that you will accept my offer of the house ?"

" I cannot take it as a gift, Albert ;" replied Aylmine, with a blush.

" Will you keep it in trust for me ?" urged Albert, " and let Winken take care of the money, plate, and furniture."

" You must not trust Winken Kroots where money is concerned. I know that he has so little command over himself, that any means, however despicable, he will stoop to—to gain possession of it.—It is his soul, life, and god !"

" Will you not then take it under your charge ?" appealed Albert.

" I will," returned the maiden, " and I know my power, and I will not hesitate to acknowledge it, over Winken Kroots ; that you may be assured if I say we will take your very kind offer, it will be done."

" And you will accept it ?" asked Albert.

No. 1. 6   G

" I will," said Aylmine.

" You are all kindness, Aylmine," replied Albert. "You do not know what a weight you have taken off my spirits by accepting my offer. I could not have rested if you had remained, for I should feel very wretched at the prospect of any harm coming to you, and—"

Here he was interrupted by voices outside the door, and he said—

" It must be the Authorities come with your—with Winken Kroots," he could not say " your father."

The fact was soon decided by his hearing the voice of Winken, calling at the foot of the stairs—" Mynheer Vanderdecken ! Mynheer Vanderdecken !"

" That is your father's voice, Aylmine," said Albert, "and I must for the present bid you farewell ; think of what I have said, and if you can feel that your happiness will not be less, if it be not increased, mine will be greater by your accepting my offer."

" It is useless, Albert," returned Aylmine ; "nay, I almost think it a wickedness to disguise our feelings for each other—the very disguise giving a tacit inference that there is something to be ashamed of. I will, therefore, run the hazard of being deemed bold in saying, that your conduct to me has excited a kindly interest in me for you, and in presenting my hand as a guarantee, you may be assured that I will, in the name of my father, accept your generous offer. I know my influence over him, and can answer that he will consent to any arrangement which I may make."

" Mynheer Vanderdecken ! Mynheer Vanderdecken !" shouted Winken Kroots from below.

" I am coming," returned Albert, and continued to Aylmine, "Thanks —thanks, dear Aylmine ; I feel that, like myself, you have too great a love for truth to excite false hopes, only to dash them to the ground. For the present, farewell." He raised her hand to his lips, and imprinted a kiss upon it, descended the stairs, and found the Authorities, taking notes of the position of the bodies and of the place. He plainly and briefly related the occurrences, which were taken down ; and the bodies were removed. Albert and Winken Kroots were then left alone, and the former observed that Aylmine had something to communicate to him, which, when Winken heard, he trotted into his house, with some vague idea that some of his property might have vanished. His mind was, however, soon set at rest by Aylmine, who stated the offer which Albert had made, and backed it by arguments, as she felt convinced he was unequal to withstand ; and Albert, who was walking up and down the outside of the house, was called in by Winken, to be thanked for the offer which he had made. That night a vehicle went backwards and forwards from Winken's residence to Albert's, containing and conveying the medicines and furniture, even to the strong box which bore the money. And when the morning sun shone upon Holland, Winken Kroots with Aylmine had taken up their abode with Albert Vanderdecken.

CHAPTER. VI.

RESTORATION OF THE CLOSED CHAMBER TO ITS PRIMITIVE NEATNESS.—ALBERT SEEKS A SHIP.

WHEN that morning sun, of which we have just spoken, had attained its highest altitude, the chamber which had such mysterious and eventful incidents connected with it, had, under the hands of Aylmine, been set in order ; the chairs had been rubbed and dusted, the carpet swept, the pictures carefully wiped, the chimney ornaments cleaned, and the silver plate, consisting of flagons, goblets, dishes, jugs, and various domestic utensils, were repolished and placed in order. And why was all this labour to produce this change in the appearance of the room bestowed ? Was it a love of cleanliness and order, alone ? Ah, no ! the pride of neatness, the desire of comfort, and the wish to see an air of good arrangement prevailing, was not the sole influence which made this extraordinary change the apartment exhibited : there was one whose eye was to be pleased, and whose grateful sympathy was to be excited, and through those means the gloom and grief hanging over him, like a heavy cloud, was to be alleviated. Aylmine had given her heart to Albert ; it was no light transient feeling which excited her imagination in his favour. She inherited all the warmth of the race from which she sprung, and she loved with all the enthusiasm of a young girl's first love—a deep devotedness to death. It had arisen from the noble delicacy and the manliness of his conduct, rather than to the beauty of his person, although that was of a nature "framed to make woman false," and perhaps assisted the imagination when dwelling on the perfections of the mind ; it was a fact she would scarcely acknowledge to herself, yet she was perfectly conscious of its existence, and garnered it up in her heart, as the dearest, most cherished object her life had yet presented to her. She had completed her task of arranging the room, and she turned round to survey it with a mingled feeling of satisfaction at the change she had made, and of melancholy, when she remembered the grief it had caused. While absorbed in reflections, partly gloomy and partly of a pleasing nature ; for Albert's image was mixed up with every thought she possessed, her father's voice broke upon her ear—

" And so," he cried, " this is the chamber which has been closed for so many years. How very odd ! What very nice furniture ; very old-fashioned, but remarkably good tho'. Handsome china ornaments ; these came from China, I can see, richly worked in gold ; ah, very nice. It is very odd—I always thought the widow was so very poor—I was told so, and believed it from her appearance. Ah, she was a careful woman—a good, prudent woman—I have no doubt ; and Albert said he was very rich, did'nt he Aylmine ?"

Aylmine nodded assent.

" Ah," continued the old man, " she must have been a very very pru-

dent woman. Why, Allah! here's a beaufet full of silver—all silver!"
and the old man took out the articles and examined them. "All mas-
sive silver too, richly carved: these are of good value. Does Albert know
their value?—I should like to buy some of him—I can't afford to give
much for them, but I dare say that the money will be more to his taste
than this old-fashioned plate. I'll go and ask him."

"You need not trouble yourself, father;" said Aylmine, stopping him
as he prepared to leave the chamber to carry his intention into effect.
"Mynheer Vanderdecken has more money than you have, therefore it
is not an object to him, and I know he will not part with them; he prizes
them as having belonged to his parents, and I would not hurt his feelings, nor shall you, by asking him to part with anything which he has an
attachment for."

"Very well!" returned Winken, "if you think he would ask more
money than I could afford to give, of course I will not ask him; but you
say that he has got a great deal of money—that he is very rich. Have
you seen his wealth? Do you know where he keeps his money?"

"No," answered Aylmine, "nor shall I ask him; what right have we
to be inquisitive upon a point which cannot concern us?"

"Yes! yes!" said Winken Kroots, "but you say that he is going
away, and we are to have charge of the house. If he has such a very
large sum of money, he cannot take it all with him; and, therefore, he
must leave it behind him, eh? We'll take care of it for him, eh! Ho!
ho! ho! I say, we'll take care of it." Aylmine was about to reply,
with an expression of scorn flashing in her eyes, when Albert entered the
room. He started when he saw Winken Kroots and Aylmine, as though
he had expected to find the room untenanted; but when he looked around
and saw the change, the air of order and comfort which prevailed, he felt
a sensation of grateful pleasure, for he understood for whom and why it
had been done. He turned to Aylmine, and taking her hand, which
he pressed kindly, he said—

"Where, Aylmine, shall I find words to thank you for this wonderous
change from desolation and discomfort to its very reverse. Were you
an enchantress you could not have effected a greater and more gratifying
change than I see around me."

"Her mother was an enchantress," interrupted Kroots.

"An enchantress?" echoed Albert, with surprise and almost a
smile.

"My mother learned to work spells from a powerful magician," replied Aylmine; "but they were all harmless in their operation, and good
in their purport. Amongst the higher and most favoured classes in the
East, it is a science much cultivated."

"Can you get any one to believe in the truth of the doctrine?" asked
Albert, still smiling. Did any of the predictions, or whatever was the
result of the mystic charms called into action, ever, by a happy coinci-
dance, come to pass?"

"Oh dear, yes!" cried Winken. "I have often been an inquirer
into futurity, and have generally found that everything predicted occurred. Aylmine's mother, as I have told you, could read futurity; and

through her possession of that extraordinary gift I saved my life and my money many times."

" Can this be true ?" asked Albert, with amazement.

" Can you doubt it ?" returned Aylmine, with a gravity almost approaching solemnity. " You, who have already by your own acknowledgment, been subject to a mystery which has an insurmountable influence upon your destiny ?"

" You are right, Aylmine," returned Albert, with a gloom overshadowing his features. " There are mysteries in nature which are inscrutable and unfathomable to us weak mortals."

" I know that there is truth in the power to foretel certain circumstances. It is true, they are told in generalities, and not in individual occurrences; but, from the aspect they wear, you may gather what is to take place; and why I know that there is truth in the power to do this, is that my mother taught me the charm; but I have not practised it for years, and may have forgotten some portion, which might prevent me succeeding were I now to try."

" For heaven's sake do not attempt it ! In this country we are expressly forbidden by our Holy Church to practise those devilish arts, and to avoid all who practise them. We are under the surveillance of the Priest here, who comes in at all times and all hours ; and were he to know that you, or any belonging to you, practised sorcery under my roof, and apparently with my sanction, I should be excommunicated; and I almost shudder to think what your fate might be."

" You forget, Albert, that this country is not under the domination of your church," returned Aylmine; " and therefore I am not so liable to a dreadful fate as you seem to consign me to."

" You know not the power, Aylmine, that we possess," said Albert, earnestly; " I pray you not to test it, although I much doubt the possibility of what you affirm."

" I do not fear the denunciation or the wrath of the Church, Albert," said Aylmine, " for I do not mean to test it, as you say ; but there are mysteries and miracles in your church, and why should your faith in them, which are unaccountable to human understanding, prevent a credence to other things, which are not more mysterious and extraordinary than those you have implicit belief in ?"

" I could easily answer your argument, by saying that they were performed by Almighty interposition, which puts them beyond all question ; that they were engines to prove the heavenly nature of the doctrines advanced ; a spiritual authority for the sanctity and divinity of the Holy Word ; and not for the mere purpose of gratifying a weak curiosity—a vain desire in poor human nature, to know what is to come. But let us drop this subject, and let me again thank you for the pains and labour you have bestowed to chase away the gloomy reflections which the recent appearance of this room excited. I can well appreciate the motive which has produced this ; and, trust me, I will do my best to deserve it ;" and taking Aylmine's hand, he led her from the room to the opposite one, where breakfast had been spread with neatness and care. Winken Kroots feasted his eyes upon the silver plate in the beaufet in the room which the couple had just quitted, and made a running calculation as to the value, and the probable sum which Albert might be induced to take for them ; and in case of his consenting to part with them for the imagined sum, what amount of profit he should clear by the bargain.　He rubbed his hands with satisfaction at the anticipated purchase, and upon cogitating as to the best time to make the offer to Albert, he recollected that he was about to leave to go to sea, perhaps never to return, and all this silver was to be left in his charge.　He rubbed his hands with greater glee than before, and rejoiced that he had not made the offer to Albert."

"There is no necessity now !　Ho !　ho !　ho !" he laughed, with a chuckling gurgle ;　"it may become mine—he's no relations—he !　he ! he !　and cost me nothing.　Good, good !" and he gazed—gloated on the plate as though he could draw it from the beaufet and hug it to his bosom with intense delight.　His joyous reverie was broken in upon by hearing his name called by Albert ; and leaving the room with reluctance, casting many " a longing, ling'ring look behind," he entered the parlour, and seated himself at the breakfast table with Albert and Aylmine.

"That is very handsome plate, Mynheer Vanderdecken, which your mother has left you," was the first remark the little gold-worshipper made on seating himself.

"I have scarce looked at it," replied Albert, indifferently.

"Dear me, how odd," returned Winken.　"I should have looked at it if it had been mine, or I had been you, from morning till night.　I am fond of those sort of richly-worked articles."

"But as it is not yours, and I am not you, such an event is not likely to take place," remarked Albert, rather angrily, annoyed by the cupidity of the little miser; but fancying that Aylmine looked pained by the harshness of his reply, he continued, in an altered tone, " but there is one thing that is yours, and that is the amount of your bill, which I promised you.　Here," he exclaimed, drawing a well filled purse from his belt, and exhibiting a large quantity of guilders to the sparkling eyes of Winken, who grinned as he gazed on them ;　"here," he said, " is the four guilders, I promised you."

"Thank you, Mynheer Vanderdecken," he cried, as he stretched his long, bony fingers, and almost snatched the coin from the extended hand of Albert, as though he feared the latter might alter his mind. "Thank you ;　I knew you would keep your word ;　l said as much to Aylmine.　Did I not, child ?"

Aylmine averted her head and spoke not a word.　Albert could easily perceive the whole transaction on the part of Winken had excited excessive disgust, and he therefore changed the conversation and said—

"I shall go to the quay to seek for a vessel bound to the East Indies, and, if I can meet with one, take a passage at once."

"When do you purpose going ?" asked Aylmine, and her heart beat as she asked the question.

"To-day," said Albert.

"So soon, so very soon," inquired Aylmine with surprise.

" Yes," returned Albert, " it is better that it should be as soon as possible ; it will be better for my peace of mind.,'

" Your peace of mind ?" echoed Aylmine.   " What need is there of your quitting your home?   You have wealth enough to make you above the cares of the world ; and —" she checked herself.

" Pray proceed," urged Albert. ·

" I was about to conclude," she continued, " that you have mental and personal qualifications to make a happy home for the being whom Providence may give to you, to spend the remainder of your days with ; and, therefore, why quit your home ?"   As she concluded, her face and neck exhibited a blush of crimson.

" It is an imperative duty which I have sworn to fulfil," answered Albert.   Aylmine dropped her head and remained silent.   Those last words fell like ice upon her heart ; it was a disappointment ; she felt a sadness on her spirits, and felt that it would be a joy to weep, and yet she scarcely knew why.   Albert also remained silent ; he felt the full force of Aylmine's remark, and the effect his reply had produced ; he thought with bitterness upon the wretched destiny to which he was doomed, with all the means of worldly enjoyment and happiness in his grasp ; and yet, Tantalus like, was forbidden by mysterious circumstances to taste them.   The silence was preserved for a short time, for the intelligence of Albert's instant departure in quest of a ship had had its influence upon Winken Kroots, it had set him cogitating ; he already saw the gilders and the silver plate in his possession.   Turning suddenly to Albert, he demanded—

" Have you any relations, Mynheer Albert ?"

" An uncle—my mother's brother," replied Albert, as if awakening out of a dream.

" Does he visit you often ?" inquired the little doctor.

" No, returned Albert, I have not seen him for some years, I know not if he is alive; and if he is, I am sure he knows not whether I am or not."

" Humph !" said Winken Kroots.   " You mean to go to sea, Mynheer Vanderdecken ?"

" I do," was the reply, gloomily given.

" Well," continued the doctor, " I approve your plan.   Your sea life is the only life for a lad of spirit; I always thought so—before I tried it, and after I left it."

" You," said Albert, with surprise ;   " were you ever a sailor ?"

" Yes," returned Winken ;   "when quite a lad I served on board a trading vessel to the East Indies."

" Ah !" cried Albert, earnestly ;   " did you ever meet with —" he checked himself, and continued.   " How long is it since you served ?"

" Let me see," reflected Winken ;   " about fifty-three or fifty-four years ago !"

" Oh !" replied Albert, and muttering to himself, " then he could not have seen it," relapsed into his former indifference.

" Ah !" continued Winken, " the sea is the sphere of action for a young man.   He goes to foreign countries, sees their manners and customs; he lives a life of action and constant excitement; the labour is not great and the payment is very fair, while board and lodging is found you. If you have much money—like you, Mynheer Albert—if it is little, or very much—I think you said yours was a very great sum—did you not?" Albert nodded assent, and the old man continued, rubbing his hands, "Yes, a very great sum—why you can leave it with some friend who will take every care of it—like me, Mynheer. Yours is a large sum; you cannot take it with you—you can leave it with us —you will not want money at sea; we will take every care of it; you can count it before you depart, we will mind it. You'll leave it with me, will you not, Albert? I beg you pardon, Mynheer Vanderdecken, I should have said.

Albert could not help smiling; he could easily see through the motive of Winken's persuading him to follow the sea, and the desire he had to get possession of the money; and he recollected the difference of Winken's behaviour to him so short a time since, when the little miser believed that he had not a guilder to boast of; and now to beg his pardon for a trifling familiarity, which Albert rather courted than felt any annoyance at. However, he replied—

"When I leave here, Mynheer Winyen Kroots, to join whatever ship I am to sail in, I shall leave whatever money I may have left, besides any other valuables which may be mine at that period, in the charge of Aylmine."

"Yes, yes," replied Winken, its all the same; we will be most careful of them. How do you yeep your money—in a chest? I should like to see how you pack a very large sum—can't you show it me?"

"Father," said Aylmine, who had aroused upon hearing her name mentioned by Albert, "you have several patients to visit this morning; unless you go at once you will lose your fees."

"Yes," said Winken; "but there is time to see the money."

"No," observed Albert, "not now, some other time."

"Very well, Mynheer Albert, some other time. You never break your word, you know; that will do, good-morning. You go to find a ship to-day; when will you sail—to-morrow, or next day?"

"Pray go, father, and ask no further questions now," said Aylmine, almost turning him out of the room; and as she returned to Albert, gazing on him with a full but melancholy glance, said—

"You are determined to quit this spot, Albert; may I inquire the cause of this extraordinary desire to leave your birthplace, with the possession of sufficient wealth to make it a happy home to live and end your days in?"

"Aylmine, do not impute so mean a feeling to me," cried Albert, with warmth, "as to imagine that I could not make this a happy home without the wealth you speak of. Do not suppose for an instant that money could at any time have any influence upon my conduct—I scorn such an idea. I have told you that there is an extraordinary mystery which hangs over me, which will either doom me to a speedy death, or a roving, wandering life, while I have existence. This I have sworn, if it should be necessary, to undergo, until I have accomplished the object to which my life will be devoted; and I acknowledge deeply the kindness of

Departure of Vanderdeeken.

your motive, which induces you to persuade me to forego my purpose fearing disaster, grief, and miserable vicissitudes, may encircle me ; but these I am prepared to meet, and remember, Aylmine, I am the only one to suffer. I leave behind me none to watch wearyingly for my return, with all the sickness of suspense and hope. My mother, Heaven rest her soul ! is no more ; and when I am far away there will be none to lament my absence, or my death, should I meet with it in fulfilling my oath."

"Albert !" exclaimed Aylmine, reproachfully, while the tears stood in her eyes, "you wrong me much in your words—you do me an injustice, I will not say an unkindness, although I—but no matter. Can you suppose that I can look upon you coldly, or even indifferently, when to you I am indebted for being saved from a fate I shudder to think upon, to which death is a thousand times to be preferred—to you, who rescued my father—I must call Winken Kroots father, for, be his faults what they may, and they only spring from one source, he has acted as a father to me, and I respect him as such—you rescued him from poverty, if not from death ; do you think I can remember this and feel no gratitude —feel no interest in one who has risked his life for mine ? Indeed, Albert, I am not so heartless ; and were your mother alive, she would not watch more anxiously for your return, or weep more sincerely for

No. 7.   H your loss, than Aylmine. You have wronged my nature, Albert—indeed you think too meanly of me," and she burst into a passion of tears. Albert sprung to her side, and earnestly exclaimed—

"Dear Aylmine, forgive me! I meant not to wound your feelings. Good God! I could not dream of such a thing. Aylmine, I cannot disguise it—I love you—dearly, sincerely love you—and it is that knowledge which adds to my anguish, when I think I must part with you. I do not ask if you return my affection, I fear it—yes, I fear it—Aylmine; for I cannot misunderstand the many little kindnesses, the looks, the gentle tenderness you have shown me, and which has added deeply and strongly to my adoration for you ; but when I remember that I am doomed by oath to a life of uncertainty, of difficulty and danger, I have strived to stifle my passion, ere I thought you could perceive it, for I thought my own demerits would prevent your conceiving any affection for me ; and I love you too well, too sincerely, to wish you to unite your fate with one whose destiny may bring you nothing but protracted anxiety and wretchedness."

"Albert, listen to me," said Aylmine, faintly, and raising her eyes to his as she removed them from her hands, in which they had been buried, " I have already told you my history, and you know that I have passed my life, from my fifth year, in little or no society but that of Winken Kroots ; I know not if I am doing wrong in giving utterance to what I am about to disclose, but you will pardon me if I am, for the motive which induces me to act thus. Since I have lost my mother I have had nothing on which to place my affections ; a native of the East, my feelings are warm and fervent, and the emotions which Winken Kroots raised in my breast, were but those of gratitude for his kindness to my poor mother and myself. Chance or destiny has thrown us together, and the circumstances which have transpired have excited such lively emotions of gratefulness that I cannot help their merging into a much kinder feeling towards you. Albert, let my candour be my pardon if I forget what is due to maidenly delicacy, if I tell you I love you, truly and devotedly; that I have never felt for mortal what I feel for you. The sacrifice of my life would be an offering of poor value compared to the estimation of the service I think you worthy of ; that I would go with you through danger, desolation, sickness and health ; cling to you when the extremest devotion was needed by you ; in truth, Albert, I love you as only woman can love ; my heart, soul, and spirit, are invested in thee ; and, be the circumstances what they may in future, I can never change—can never cease to love you with an undying attachment."

"Aylmine, dear, dearest Aylmine!" exclaimed Albert, passionately, and extending his arms, she sunk weeping upon his breast. Albert pressed her to his bosom, and felt a mingled sensation of extreme delight, and yet an overpowering sensation of melancholy oppress him. " I will not wrong her innocent confession," he thought, " for ten thousand worlds ; I will confide my secret to her ; and if, when she knows it, and the oath I have taken, to fulfil the line of duty marked out for me to pursue, she will unite her fate with mine, we will be wedded ; and may Almighty God, whose ways are wisdom, prosper our union." At this juncture Father Francis entered the room, Winken Kroots having, when he departed, left the door unfastened. He started as he beheld the position of the two lovers, and exclaimed—

"The Holy Virgin save you, my son!" He looked hard and earnestly at Aylmine, who upon his entrance had hastily disengaged herself from the arms of Albert. "May I inquire," he continued, still addressing Albert, "who this young maiden is; I have never seen her before?"

"It is the daughter of Winken Kroots, the doctor, Holy Father;" replied Albert. "They have both, at my very earnest request, taken up their abode here."

"Thy motive in making the offer was, I trust, a good and virtuous one, my son," said the father, looking, with a suspicious glance towards Aylmine. "I hope that your own bosom will not impugn it, nor you have any cause to regret having done so."

"I do not fear it, father; and I had hoped you knew my character too well to have even imagined I could have been guilty of such baseness as your allusion points at," replied Albert, proudly; "and for Aylmine, her very appearance must place her immediately above all suspicion."

"My good child," said the father, "I would not wrong that young tender maiden by so impure a thought; and although I know your character better, my son, than you do yourself, and can attach a greater value to it than you would, yet I know the weakness of human nature too well to trust to the best intentions and most virtuous motives where two young fond hearts are concerned. Two beings who are all in all, the whole world to each other, can seldom consider what is prudent and proper in the hour of temptation and passion, and but too often commit an act which becomes a crime in one light, where custom makes it a virtue in another. If you are not betrothed you should be—aye, even married. It is not seemly that you should remain longer living 'neath the same roof, and act as I have seen you, without such ceremony being performed. Believe me, maiden, the female who grants the first liberty without resistance, finishes by granting more than she ever dreamed would be asked for."

"Father, what you say is wise and instructive," said Albert, "although, I confess, I felt it an intrusion; and pardon me, father, almost an impertinence; but a moment's cool reflection teaches me that you are right. I love Aylmine, dearly and tenderly; she has just confessed an interest beyond a kindly feeling for me; I will plight my troth—I will wed her, cheerfully, delightedly, this very instant; but there is an objection—a very great objection—in the way. It remains for her to say whether it is an insuperable one; if she does not think so, I am her's while on earth, only and alone. It is a secret which you desired to learn upon your first visit to me after my mother's death I refused to disclose it to you then, for I knew it not all. Now I am acquainted with as much as it is possible for me to know: it is in this secret lies my determination to go to sea, and in that lies the objection to my wedding Aylmine. I must tell Aylmine all. I also intended to confide it in your breast, father, and no opportunity can be better than the present to relate it."

"Speak on, my child; the Holy Virgin will give me strength to counsel you in this strait," said Father Francis; "and I will endeavour, to the best of my poor ability, to so advise thee, that thy worldly welfare and happiness shall be cared for, and thy spiritual comfort considered."

Albert then related to the wondering Aylmine and the pious Father every incident connected with the closed apartment, and with his father; of the means pointed out to him by which the term of his erring parent's punishment might be abated; and of the oath which he had sworn upon the sacred relic to fulfil the object, even if he perished in the attempt.

"This, Father, is all that has transpired, and it now rests with Aylmine whether we should be united in the holy state of matrimony, or part now, and perhaps for ever. What say you, Father?"

"It is strange and mysterious!" replied Father Francis. "The signs you have mentioned; your mother's perturbed state of mind whenever that room was spoken of; its influence on her life, and causing her death, all unite in leading me to believe there is much awful truth in what you have told me. For your line of action, which you are to pursue, I am sorry you should have so rashly made an oath, which sprung from excitement of the mysteries around, and which mysteries might have been caused by an evil spirit, as well as from the apparent cause. Whether it is right you should keep your oath or be absolved from it, I cannot at this moment determine; but will, this night, in solemn prayer, request to be shown how to guide you. With regard to the maiden, her course must be guided by her own judgment. If she cannot, now she is made acquainted with the strange circumstance in which your fate is wrapped up, bear its incertitude, its disappointment, its cares and anxiety, with which it will be encompassed, if I should esteem it necessary to advise the fulfilment of your oath, you had both far better part now—at once, and for ever!"

"No! no! no!" cried Aylmine, who spoke for the first time since the priest's entrance. "I cannot part for ever, Albert. You would not leave me—it would break my heart;" and she sobbed violently. The excitement she had undergone in the first instance when she disclosed her affection, her first and dearest love, and after that the intense interest with which she had listened to the recital of Albert, and now the alternative—to part for ever, being presented to her, was too much for her already overstrained nerves to bear, and she wept like a child on Albert's bosom. He used every effort to console and soothe her, and at length she raised her head, and, placing her right-hand in Albert's, she exclaimed, "Albert, it is left for me to decide whether we should be united by laws of man, to make valid and virtuous the law of nature, which binds our hearts so strongly together—it is left to me, with a generous motive, which I estimate proudly and dearly, to say whether I will bind myself—through good and evil, while life exists in one or both—to one whom a cruel and relentless destiny has doomed to a wandering, uncertain, and dangerous life. Albert, how should a woman show her love, her devotion, to the object she adores, if it is not in danger, in sickness, in despair, and misery; she can cling to him, console him in his wretchedness, tend him, and be a guardian spirit to him in pain and difficulty? Albert, were this mysterious situation in which you are placed of a far greater amount of probable misery, I would be thine thine—as I am now, for ever—while life is a portion of this frail tenement!"

" Bless thee! bless thee! Dear, sweet Aylmine!" energetically ejaculated Albert.   " May I wither, heart and soul, if I abuse thy confidence !"

The Father felt the tears fill his eyes as he witnessed the plighting the troth of the two young hearts, and he silently prayed that they might be spared the griefs and disappointments of this cold world, although they anticipated them ;   and bestowing his blessing on them, and telling Albert that he would in the morning tell him how to proceed with regard to his oath, he crossed the threshold and passed out, leaving them again alone. For two succeeding hours they enjoyed each others' society in sweet converse, which, though as delightful to them as Paradise to angels, would be tedious in the recital.

In good time Winken Kroots returned, and Albert took him into the chamber which had been the scene of so many events, and showing him the whole of the plate, and next the large chest, which he opened and displayed the hoard of guilders, he proposed to him, as her guardian, for the hand of Aylmine.   The sight of the money quite took away the breath of the little miser, and on the question being repeated, he seized Albert by the hand, and would have embraced him, had he suffered him, gaving his full consent with an expression of the greatest delight and joy. He muttered something about going to sea, about the money being left in his charge, and the absence of any necessity of his giving Aylmine a dowry as Albert was so rich, and should they put their money in one chest to take care of it, and a hundred other things, which Albert would not answer; but locking his chest, and putting it away, and locking his beaufet, he politely handed Mynheer out of the chamber.

In a few minutes he was on his way to the docks, and on inquiry ascertained that a vessel, belonging to the Dutch East India Company, would sail in about a month from that time.   Albert inquired the residence of the Captain, and easily found the place he was directed to ;   the Captain was at home, and in an interview which Albert had with him, the Captain agreed to take Albert the voyage there and back, and teach him seamanship :   and when the preliminaries were arranged, the agreement entered into, and everything settled, the Captain promised to give Albert timely notice of the departure of the vessel ;   and, taking his leave, the latter returned dull and dispiritedly to his own abode.   He detailed to Aylmine the result of his interview; he pointed out to her the short time they were likely to remain near each other, and begged her to name an early day for their wedding.   Aylmine was not a female to be affected by false delicacy, and in three days from that day—

> " In the lustre of her youth, she gave
> Her hand with her heart in it"

to Albert.

CHAPTER. VII.

THE PILOT.

TIME, when pleasantly occupied, flies past swiftly and unnotedly, and Albert found that the period succeeding his marriage had flown away as rapidly as it was delightful ; he had even forgotten that a time would arrive when the charm would be broken, and he must leave the being he so dearly loved, perhaps never again to meet.   His recollection was painfully awakened one morning by seeing a man, in the garb of a seaman, standing in the middle of the room, in which himself and Aylmine were seated upon the sofa.   Their knowledge of the man's presence arose from his uttering in a sharp harsh voice, " Mynheer Albert Vanderdecken." Albert and Aylmine both started as though a spectre had arisen and stood before them.   They had not heard him enter, and were, therefore, to say the least, much surprised at his presence.   Albert gazed on him, and his scrutiny terminated with anything but a feeling of satisfaction.   The stranger was not a short man, and yet appeared so from a contracted stoop of the shoulders ; his limbs were powerful, and his arms hung loosely by his side, his hands half-open ; he had long black matted hair, thick bushy eyebrows, a profusion of black whiskers, and his features were strongly marked, bearing an expression painful to behold.   They had the appearance of having obtained their character from wretchedness and bitterness, or from foul and malignant passions.   His complexion was white to deathliness, and contrasting with the deep black of his whiskers gave his features a ghastly hue, terrible to behold.   Albert almost shuddered as he asked—

" Who, and what are you ?   How gained you admission to this apartment, without my being aware of it until you addressed me by name ?"

" My name is Paul Sachs—I am a pilot.   I found the outer door and that of this room open ; I walked in ; if you heard me not, you must be deaf, or I walk lighter than other people.   Ho ! ho !" said the stranger, and concluded with a grating laugh.

" What is your business with me ?" demanded Albert, somewhat nettled by the sneering tone of the stranger.

" I have brought you a letter from my captain ; I belong to the ship you are going to sail in.   Here," and he proffered a sealed packet to Albert, who eagerly snatched it and broke the seal, and commenced reading the contents with great avidity.

" Is he to sail soon ?" timidly asked Aylmine.

" Too soon to please you, I suppose, come when it will," gruffly retorted the man.   " It is the way with you women, you would keep a man from acting like a man if you had your own way ; always fondling, and prattling, and playing, like babies, but you have got a snug place too, and there are many comforts ; ah, and luxuries too, to leave behind, for the pleasure of sailing on the blue water.   Well, if I had a snug berth like this, and a pretty wife to boot, I should not be so ready to box about on salt water.   You're a young wife; you won't like to lose your husband so soon after marriage, eh ? but you'll get other lovers, its the way with you all.   Ho ! ho ! ho !"

" You presume, Sir !" said Aylmine, offendedly, and turned away. She looked over Albert's shoulder, and inquired the contents of the letter.

" It is a letter from the captain, requesting me to join him in three days.   The notice is short he allows, but understanding that I was recently wedded, he would not break in upon my felicity by so disagreeable

OR THE DEMON SHIP.

a communication, until the latest moment; and even now they sail rather earlier than was intended, from the prevalence of a fair wind, and being quite ready for sea. I shall keep the appointment, you will tell the Captain," he cried, turning to the spot were the pilot had stood, but he was gone; and his sudden absence created almost as extraordinary a sensation, as his sudden appearance had done.

" Where is the man ?" was the question which naturally rose to the lips of Albert.

" Gone, as he came, in the same strange manner," replied Aylmine, " without salutation, without sound."

" It is very strange," said Albert, thoughtfully.

" It is but a portion of the mystery which encircles you, dear Albert," returned Aylmine. " That man is some way connected with it, I am sure. Did you not feel the air grow cold as you became aware of his presence ? Has it not returned to its original warmth since his departure ?"

" I did," said Albert, " to an extreme, as though every vein in my body was on the point of freezing ; but would not mention it, for I thought it might be but fancy."

" It was no fancy," answered Aylmine; " but let us leave such speculations, and converse upon what is nearer to my heart. Have you heard from Father Francis ? has he advised you respecting the fulfilment of your oath ?"

" He has," replied Albert. " I saw him on my way to seek a ship. He told me he had consulted a learned Superior, and his advice—and his own reflections upon the extraordinary occurrences which had taken place had induced him to coincide with it—was, that I should proceed upon my first voyage ; and that if during that journey I met with nothing which applied to the strange mission I was on, I should give up all thoughts of proceeding with it until I had some sign or token which might induce me to further investigate it. As this was congenial to my own feelings upon the subject, I have acted upon it, and have proceeded thus far with it.'

" I fear, Albert, there is too much truth in the whole affair, and the mysterious visit of the seaman, is one sign that you must go on with it," said Aylmine, mournfully. " You will do me the justice, I know, to believe how my heart will be wrung by your absence. It is such anguish that I dare not think of it; but I would not let it interfere with the terrible duty you have to perform, even though I feel I should die if you leave me ; yet I cannot deny that I experience some consolation in a strong belief that pervades me, that I shall see you again—that your object will not be accomplished this time, and that though you may meet with danger and difficulties during your voyage, yet you will come back to me as unharmed in person and free and gentle in heart as you are now."

" And ever will be, as far as my heart and affection for you, dear Aylmine, are concerned," cried Albert, warmly. " Believe me, I feel our separation more deeply on your account than I do on my own, if it were possible. That I love you dearly and devotedly, I swear by all my fondest hopes and thoughts. But, ere I saw you, I was partly acquainted with the mystery that drags me from everything which can give a charm to life. I was alone in the world, the depositary of a fearful secret, which concerned me nearly and dearly. I knew that my fate must, if I spent my life in the awful search to which I felt myself bound, be one of a wandering, restless, and perhaps a wretched nature. I had prepared my mind to endure it, be it whatever it might be, and I had no one to leave behind me who could care or shed a tear for me, died I when and wherever it pleased heaven to will it. I had schooled myself to quit, with little regret, a place which possessed only painful recollections for me; when, like a star which sheds its lustre from one drear canopy of cloud, you broke upon my sight, and from the first moment I beheld you I gave you my heart. I strove to conceal it from you, for I knew to what I was doomed, and to what wretchedness you might be consigned were I to gain your affections, and then to be compelled, after a brief period, to quit you for years—perhaps for ever; and I resolved that I would not act thus to you; whatever amount of suffering I might endure, it would be but adding to the general stock. But I found, good as my intentions were, I could not act upon them—I could not disguise from you that I loved you; and you, dear Aylmine, who had been kept from all but the sight of Winken, construed one or two little acts of duty with an affectionate kindness into a worth they did not deserve, and looked upon me with a feeling far beyond my merit, and, trusting your imagination rather than your judgment, consigned to my keeping the richest, noblest gift a man can receive—the loving and affectionate heart of a young and innocent maiden. In this instance, Aylmine, your imagination deceived you. You invested me with attributes I do not possess, and you looked probably forward to a life of domestic quiet and happiness, which, so judge me Heaven as I speak true, should, had I been by fate permitted, have been my study and object in life. I can therefore deeply and strongly appreciate how you will feel this cruel breaking-up of your anticipated happiness, and I shall bear with me more unhappy recollections of what you will suffer when I am gone, than I can from any misfortune which may befal me, of however great magnitude."

" You speak and act as you have ever done, my dearest husband, to me," said Aylmine, fondly and energetically, " with the extremest kindness and consideration ; but you do me a wrong if you suppose that my imagination had only pictured to me a bright side of life with you. It took but a short time to become assured that, as far as you were concerned, my happiness would be as great as any woman can hope or desire ; but, dear Albert, I had already passed through vicissitudes, and you had nobly, ere you offered me your hand, acquainted me with the singular and mysterious situation in which you were placed with the oath that you made, and of your intention of religiously keeping it. This I knew ; I could not, therefore, be surprised or disappointed, however grieved I might be, that a time would arrive when I must probably part with you and my affection for you, believe me, was not to be controlled by your concealing from me that you loved me. I could not love anything base or mean-spirited; but I could love the being who possessed true nobility of character, although that being had never attempted to gain my

Trepidation of Mynheer Peter Von Schmidt at the familiarity of the bear.

affection ; you, therefore, attach an undue value to my feelings, and too little to your own, in speaking as you have but now. To part with you, Albert, is like parting with my heart-strings ; but my anguish does not arise from a disappointed hope of happiness, but because I love you dearly and tenderly ; and do not, I entreat you, depart with a supposition that my unhappiness arises from a blighted hope. We shall meet again —I feel it—I know it, and until then I will strive to bear up as proudly as becomes the wife of him who has nobly bent himself to a task fraught with danger and misery, rather than swerve from that stern line of duty which his honour and filial reverence have pointed out to him."

" God bless thee, dear Aylmine !" said Albert, while the tears of strong feeling stood in his eyes, and extending his arms, he enfolded Aylmine in them, as she wept on his bosom.

" Always billing and cooing—always billing and cooing!" cried Winken Kroots, entering at the same moment. "Ah—ah—a time will come when all that will end—it has its day—make the most of it."

" That day has come," said Albert, trying to smile. " I am going to leave you sooner than even you expected."

" Going to leave us sooner than even I expected?" echoed Winken, rather surprisedly. " Why, when are you going ?"

No. 8.   I

" The day after to-morrow," was the reply.

" Why, that is indeed soon !" cried Winken, rubbing his hands with an expression of satisfaction, which he made a faint effort to conceal. " But we shall take every care of your gold. Shall we put it all into one trunk, yours and mine ? You can count yours, and I will see that it is all safe."

" It will be quite safe in Aylmine's hands, with whom I intend to leave it," said Albert, almost harshly, at the same time wondering how it was possible such an excessive thirst of gold could exist in any being bearing a human form ; but he soon turned to other thoughts, and the short time which he could now call his own was fully employed in getting every-thing ready for his departure. The time arrived, to Albert and Aylmine with a speed like magic, and everything being placed on board the vessel, nothing was now left but for the two to part. We will spare our readers a description of the agony of the farewell, of the last embrace, and of the bearing away of the fainting form of Aylmine by Winken Kroots, who squeezed out a few tears, to his own surprise, as well as to the astonishment of some persons who saw him, and knew him. The tears came from him certainly like water compressed from a sponge which is nearly dry ; but, few as they were, they sprung from a good feeling, and they ought not to be quarreled with on that account. We usually prize rarities, and the proper value should be awarded to Winken Kroots' tears.

CHAPTER VIII.

ALBERT'S FIRST VOYAGE.

ONE of the saddest feelings we experience in life is parting from those we esteem and love with an uncertain future before us—a future of which we have no pleasing hope, no fond expectations, or bright anticipations ; leaving all that is dear and cherished—all that has excited our best and brightest wishes, brought out our better feelings, extracting our purer thoughts from the base alloy and dross with which they have been mixed —to seek strange lands, strange people, and cold hearts, on a mission which may bring us no joy, or even a latent good. This is as sad, as grievous a feeling as we can possess ; it comes like a blight upon the heart, and crushes the spirit with a bitterness which makes us wonder that human feelings can be the instruments of such mortal suffering.

When Aylmine was borne away, Albert felt as though he had parted with all and everything in the world which could produce in him a desire to live; it seemed as if every motive and necessity of existence had passed away ; and he remained a mere breathing machine—a spectre—a shadow —a human being without a soul. When he had parted from Aylmine, he quitted the deck and sought the cabin. His lip was quivering, there was a burning fire in his bosom ; his mouth was parched, and his eyes red and bloodshot ; he had shed no tears, but he felt as though he could weep a flood, if some iron barrier was removed; his throat was swollen, as though he had some mass in it, choking him ; he clenched his hands in his hair, and almost prayed for tears—yet they came not ; his heart throbbed, and was full to bursting. He tried to think of common-place things, to tear his mind from what seemed driving him on to madness— but in vain : it was like an imaginative presence of some unearthly object before his eyes, which, although he closed them to shut it out, still shone brightly on his brain. In an agony of bitterness and anguish he threw himself on his knees, and cried—

" Dear, beloved Mother! who art now amongst the blessed in Heaven; you who never looked on me with unkindness, who never spoke one harsh word to me, who was ever gentle in thought and in action to the way-ward child who did not understand the richness of the treasure, the value of what he possessed in thee, until thou wert lost to him, perhaps for ever. Let thy mild spirit breathe its influence over me, and calm my soul from the misery, the wretchedness it now endures; and, oh! as thou didst disclose the awful and mysterious circumstances connected with my pre-sent undertaking, look down upon me, and lend me strength to proceed in what I have sworn to fulfil ; and in whatever dangers, difficulties, and miserable situations it may please the Almighty power to subject me to, do thou lend thine aid to make me bear His dispensations with resigna-tion, fortitude, and humility." .

" And, Spirit of my dear, dear Mother ! as thou didst bear an affliction, an unceasing agony, from the loss of my father, until the Almighty took you to his bosom, do thou, in consideration of what thou thyself endured, shed a mild and gentle resignation and consolation, in my absence, over my young and beloved Aylmine, my dear, adored wife; who, through me, may perhaps be destined to pass the best portion of her existence in sick-ening expectation and wearying, anxious hope. Oh, hear me, dear Mo-ther ! loved and honoured while you lived, and thy memory revered and respected now that thou hast passed away." He bowed his head and clasped his hands convulsively together. He remained a short time longer in prayer, and then rising, and feeling as if the cabin was so hot that it would suffocate him, he left it and gained the deck. He bowed to the captain as he passed him, and leaning over the taffrail parted his hair from his forehead, and the cool air playing over it seemed to relieve him and bring calmness to his agitated mind. When he had obtained more possession of himself, he observed that the vessel had not yet got her anchor up, and that the fleet they were to sail in company with had al-ready weighed and stood out to sea. He therefore walked up to the cap-tain and inquired the cause of the delay. The captain had a good round oath rise to his lips, but, possibly in consideration of Albert's being an entire stranger to him, checked its utterance, and merely said that he was " waiting for the supercargo." The conversation took another turn, and Albert inquired respecting the route, and whether the danger was so great as it was usually represented in doubling the Cape. The captain gave him every information he required, as far as a rough description went, and at length to Albert's pleasure, for once on board the vessel he was most anxious to sail, the signal was given that the supercargo had left the shore on his way to the ship. He reached the vessel, and Albert saw a queer-looking little man quit the boat. Five guns were fired by way of salute, as he stepped on board the vessel ; and the Captain, followed by Albert, advanced to received him. He was dressed in a broad-skirted coat, deep plum-coloured satin knee-breeches, with gold buckles at the knees ; silk stockings, handsomely clocked ; a flowered satin waistcoat, reaching half-way down•his thighs ; a full neck-tie, and long ruffles at the wrist. Upon his head was a full-bottomed, long, curly wig, and upon that a three-cornered cocked hat, deeply edged with gold lace. He was a spare, thin man, small-featured ; having little round eyes, like black beads; a sharp, peaked nose; a small shrivelled face. He assumed much consequence, and strutted about very like the jackdaw in the peacock's feathers, so aptly described in the fable. He faintly nodded, in return for the low bow made to him by the Captain, and favoured Albert with a long stare; he, however, took no further notice of him; but requesting the Captain to let him be shown to his cabin, disappeared almost immediately after he had appeared. The capstern bars were manned, the anchor was hove up to the ship's bows, and the ship stood out of port in good style.

"Captain," said Albert, "the little supercargo assumed a very great superiority, and the salute, as well as the deference yourself and officers paid him, leads me to believe that he is of much importance. Is it so?"

"It is," returned the captain. "Their duty is to superintend the freight and trade; but the Company invest them with extraordinary powers. They presume to an extent you would hardly credit; as their account is taken before ours, and if unfavourable, is registered against us, to be produced when the vessel is next to be chartered. They know this but too well, and act accordingly. They are officers, captain, King, all in one ; and we scarcely say—in a certain point of view—that our soul's our own while they are with us."

"That must be a most disagreeable state of things," returned Albert.

"Yes," said the captain; "and you will have an opportunity of judging how much so; and the worst of it is, there exists at present no remedy for it. But let us change the subject. You will excuse me, Mynheer, but it seems an odd circumstance to me, that you, a young man with a comfortable fortune, and a very pretty wife, should leave all this ease and luxury for the uncertain wanderings and hardships of a seaman's life ; the inducement must indeed be very strong which causes this."

"I believe," said Albert, with a little embarrassment, "that no person undertakes any important action in their life without some strong and particular motive ; this is an abstract fact, of which all men must needs be aware. Were I to deny that I had not one, you would not believe me probably, I will therefore say nothing more than I am actuated by a restless desire to become a trader to the Indies. I intend, if I am spared, to purchase into the company, and in the command of one of my own vessels to sail this passage until I am satisfied." As the captain could not by any possibility understand the allusion conveyed by Albert in his last sentence, he replied—

"Until you are satisfied? Ah, young gentleman, you'll soon be that, I'll warrant you. I am thinking a rough passage round the Cape, and a two years' absence from your wife and home, will cure your love for a roving life."

" Two years !" echoed Albert, not thinking his absence from Aylmine would be of so long a duration. " Are the voyages usually that length of time ?"

" Aye, they are !" said the captain, " and very often a longer period. I have been away four or five years at a stretch, and twice have been glad to get back without ship, money, or property of any description, deeply wounded in fortune and spirit. I have, however, I am happy to say, in my last two voyages amassed a little property together, and I am in hope, if this voyage proves successful, I shall be removed from any necessity of again ploughing salt water."

" I am sure I hope your wishes may be realised," said Albert, who had felt interested in the captain's conversation ; " and should this voyage give me satisfaction sufficient to set my mind at ease—I—"

He was here interrupted by a violent ringing, proceeding from the cabin which contained the exiguous supercargo.

" There he begins," said the captain; " I wonder what he is in want of now." The ringing proceeded with great violence, and he continued, " You see, Mynheer, what he promises; perhaps you will not mind stepping to see to what quarter his wishes point."

" Certainly not," answered Albert, and proceeded at once to the cabin. On opening the door he was surprised to see Mynheer Peter Von Schmidt without his wig, exhibiting a large polished head, like a large ivory ball, and features grinning in horrible distortion, as if under the influence of the most extraordinary terror. His appearance of fright was added to by his being seated, or rather kneeling, upon the table, while he was clinging to the bell-rope, and pulling with all his might and main. Albert wondered within himself what could be the cause of his excessive alarm; and looking round the room, he perceived in one corner a bear, with the wig on his nozzle, sniffering, and sitting with all the gravity of a learned judge upon the bench. Albert could not repress his laughter at this singular scene, and Mynheer Schmidt on observing his entrance, changed his roar for help to an outcry for the captain, shouting—

" Bring arms, fire arms, cutlasses ! Cut him down ! I shall be murdered ! Help ! Where is the captain ? He shall rue this—it was done on purpose—a design to destroy me; but the Company shall know how their officer is treated on board the Johannes."

Albert proceeded to the bear, which he found a tame and harmless one, and rescuing the wig from its nose, restored it to Mynheer Von Schmidt, and turned the bear out of the cabin. Returning, he assisted the poor little frightened officer to dismount, and placed him safely upon an arm chair; for which kindness he had the satisfaction of being treated most ungraciously, and being desired in the most unceremonious and peremptory manner to quit the cabin and send the captain to him. For a moment Albert felt angry at being commanded in so upstart a manner ; but remembering that he was on board in an inferior capacity, and also recollecting the nature of the being from whom it sprung, slightly smiling, he left the cabin and went on deck. Having found the captain, he related what had passed, and of the demand made by the supercargo for his presence. The captain shrugged his shoulders, and attended to the request. He soon returned, and informed Albert that Von Schmidt had demanded that the bear should be thrown overboard, but that he had resisted in such terms, that the terrified supercargo had consented to its remaining. Albert soon became accustomed to his duties, and showing a great willingness to learn, met with a readiness to teach in those who were proficient in the duties he was required to know. His deference to those above him, and his good-natured suavity to his equals and those beneath him, created many friends, and the well-disposing of all on board—save one man, and he had shown an absence of all friendliness of feeling; kindness, or indeed any attempts at conciliation, were without avail, completely ineffectual. This man, under all and every circumstance, was cold and repulsive in his conduct to Albert, and he even fancied that he was endeavouring to excite the ship's crew against him: this man was the pilot who had summoned him to the ship, Paul Sachs. Albert could divine no cause why he should thus have excited a dislike in the man, and felt at least, however strange it may seem, that the repugnance was mutual. The man's appearance—that of living death—made him shudder whenever he saw him; and whenever chance threw them near each other, he felt that icy chilliness pervade his frame which he had experienced on their first meeting. Next to the thoughts of his wife and mission, this man excited the strongest and most constant speculations in his mind, and he frequently wondered whether any one beside himself and Aylmine felt that coldness which seemed to reign around him.

Albert was one day, while the vessel was anchored off the Table Bay, laying upon the deck, and had just fallen into a gentle slumber, when he awoke benumbed, as though he had fallen asleep upon ice. He opened his eyes, and as soon as he became conscious of surrounding objects, he perceived Paul Sachs deliberately, though cautiously, drawing the chain to which the relic was attached from his bosom: in an instant he snatched it from his hand, and springing to his feet, he demanded, with indignation, "how he dared to rifle his person."

"That is too strong a word, Mynheer," said Sachs, with a malignant tone, although a little abashed at being discovered. "I only wanted to satisfy a curiosity. As I passed you I perceived the chain round your neck, and I concluded that it was the portrait of your pretty wife, whom you left behind to enjoy herself while your were away; and as I had seen her, I only wanted to know if the miniature was like the original."

"You are mistaken, you perceive," said Albert, with asperity.

"Yes, in two things," cried the pilot, with a scornful laugh; "in that and that you are a Catholic. I thought you were a protestant: that is a piece of the Holy Cross you wear. Ho! ho! ho!"

"You are correct in your conjectures as to my being a Catholic, and that I wear a portion of the Holy Cross; you will also be correct if you conjecture that upon any future attempt of the like nature with the present, that you will be punished severely for it. Now, Sir, walk forward, if you please."

Paul Sachs eyed him with a malicious, savage glance, and uttering a jeering, yet icy laugh, he obeyed the order, and went to the forecastle. Albert followed him unconsciously to the quarter-deck, and overheard him entertaining the stragglers at the gangway with the intelligence of his being a Catholic, and of the portion of the Holy Cross, "which," he said, " was to save them all from being drowned !" As Albert felt that he could not command his temper, he quitted his place, and ascending the poop-ladder, paced up and down, striving to stifle a foreboding of evil, which the conduct and conversation of this man had given birth to.

After staying the requisite time to take cattle and water on board, the fleet sailed, the Johannes sailing in company. For a few days there was a nice breeze from the Southward and Eastward, and making decent progress, the journey became pleasant : but ere a week had elapsed, the breeze had freshened to a gale, and they had run before it so rapidly, that upon its continuance, the captain, near meridian one morning, having a clear sun, used his cross staff to discover the latitude he was in, and finding that he was too much to the Northward, he beat up to the Eastward, to get closer to the land ; and a man was sent up aloft to look for it. In a few hours the wind lulled and gradually died away, and a distant sullen sound breaking upon their ears, was accompanied by the voice of the look-out, exclaiming—

" Upon deck there !"

And the master's voice responded—

" Hallo !"

" Land, right a-head !"

" Aha," said the captain, " I thought so;" and seizing a speaking trumpet, cried—

" Foretopmast-head, there"

" Sir," said the look-out.

" What does it look like ?" cried the captain.

" Low sand-hills, with a heavy surf running," replied the man aloft.

" Steady," said the captain, to the man at wheel.

" Here, you Sir," he called to the watch on the quarter-deck, " pass the word forward for the pilot, Paul Sachs." The word was passed, and Paul came aft, with an air of pleasure in his countenance.

" Now, pilot," said the captain, " do you know this coast ?"

" Aye, Sir," he replied, " as well as I know a bowline from a clue-garnet."

" What sort of a bottom is there ?" asked the captain, anxiously.

" Why, Sir, this ground-swell, which is sweeping us rapidly in, will show you a set of teeth which will make splinters of the Johannes' bottom faster than a sixteen-pounder would a mainmast."

" Is there no way of avoiding them ?" inquired the captain, earnestly.

" No," answered the man, with a laugh, " unless a good breeze springs up suddenly dead of shore, or we were of the same stuff as the Flying Dutchman."

Albert started as he heard this name mentioned—the Phantom Ship which bore his father—and he looked at the man who had uttered the words, and found the pilot's eyes glaring on him with an indefinable expression of devilish glee, as though he could say, " I am in possession of your secret." The glance he met confused Albert, and he asked himself, " Can this mysterious man be acquainted with the purport of my voyage ? with my extraordinary secret ? It seems incredible, yet it must be so; and if so, he is of unearthly being." His speculations were interrupted by the captain ordering a man into the chains for soundings; the first heave gave fifteen fathoms.

"That sounds well," said the captain, turning to the pilot.

"Not so very well," returned he; "the water breaks in twelve fathoms. Keep her South'erd and East'erd half-sou'," he called to the man at the wheel: but it was of little use, we are sweeping bodily in, and in another hour you will see what stuff your ship's bottom 's made of."

Breakers a-head," shouted the man aloft.

They all looked, and they could see the sea running high over the breakers, and the roar increased every moment; the sailors gathered into knots on the gangway, and discoursed on the danger they were in; and the captain walked up and down, anxiously looking at the shore, and then up to see if a breeze was likely to come and assist them; but there was no satisfaction in his face, as he turned to Paul Sachs, and said—

"You must get out the boats, and see if we can't tow her off, and if any light wind springs up we may manage to clew off."

"No chance of it," said the pilot, you have'nt the boats to draw her over the current; nothing but a smart breeze can help us."

"We will try it, however," said the captain, whose anxiety visibly increased as they drew nearer to the breakers; and darkness came on as the sun sunk down in the West. He gave the necessary orders, the boats were hoisted out, the tow ropes handed in; and the captain also gave orders for provisions and various necessaries to be packed up, in case there should be no other means of escape, than by trusting to the boats, which feeble hope even Paul Sachs endeavoured to dash to the ground, by saying that they could not live in the heavy surf which broke upon the shore; things were at this awful crisis, when Philip, who had with the rest been gazing most anxiously shoreward, pointed out a change of colour in the water near the shore, and suggested that it was a breeze springing up; the captain looked in the direction, and his countenance brightening up, he cried—

"It is a breeze coming off shore! Hurrah! Come along, my beauty!" and he whistled, with the superstitious idea that the act would increase the speed and force of the coming breeze.

In a very little while the walk of the ship was increased, the helm was put up, and she soon had steerage-way on her. There was now great anxiety to know if the wind would hold steady; as yet it came in puffs, which died away, and another would spring up; still they were of sufficient force to prevent her driving on the breakers, which yet roared on the quarter. At length it came on again, and held on steadily, the boats were called in, and in an hour the Johannes was standing out to sea, freed from all present danger.

Albert and the Captain stood on the poop and conversed on their late danger.

"It would have been well for us if we had kept a wider offing—we should not have found that there is sometimes more to be feared from no wind than a regular gale," observed the Captain.

Escape of Albert and the surpercargo from the wreck of the Johannes.

"It was a narrow escape," said Albert ; "this breeze was the saving of us."

"You mean that breeze," said the Captain ; "the canvas is shaking, you see—the breeze has blown itself out : but it is of little consequence now, we are safe enough here."

"Did the little supercargo become acquainted with the chance he had of paying his devoirs to the fishes ?" asked Albert.

"Or the fishes paying their devours to him, you mean," said the Captain, laughing : "Oh, yes, I went and told him, in order that he might have the papers ready to save, if possible. At first he told me to let the ship go to pieces if I dared, he would let the Company know. Then, when he heard the breakers roaring, he became very much frightened, and insisted upon having the very largest boat that belonged to the ship for himself and papers. When I refused this, because, as I endeavoured to convince him, there were scarce boats enough to contain all the men, he grew outrageous, and said the Company should hear how their best officers were put upon and insulted by their sea captains : and when he heard the tread of the men, and the noise of hoisting out the boats, he grew horribly alarmed—his teeth chattered, and he civilly requested me to be sure and make room for him and the papers in one of

No. 9.   K

the boat. I told him he should be well cared for ; but I said that the life of every man in the ship—seaman, petty-officer, or officers—were as dear to the possessors as his could possibly be to him ; and that in a matter of life and death—as the attempted escape would be—he could not expect the same deference paid to him as when the vessel was free from any cause of alarm, and the strictest discipline preserved : I could not expect it myself, who, under any other circumstance, would be held by them as King and Lord of all and everything on board. He made me no reply ; and as I had no time to waste with him I came upon deck."

" I have noticed that he has been concocting a letter to the Company ; for, twice or thrice, when I have been in the cabin, he has read part of it aloud, and touched and retouched it. As I heard the bear mentioned several times, I concluded it was a memorial to them about you from that circumstance."

" Let him do his worst. I am in hopes this will be my last voyage," said the captain.

" I hope so, if it will bring you the accomplishment of your desires," said Albert, warmly.

" Thankye ! thankye !" answered the captain, who entertained a great friendliness for Albert; who, having paid handsomely, was treated rather as a passenger than as one of the crew. The sun rose the next morning on them completely becalmed, there was not a breath stirring ; the day passed away in the same manner. As the evening lessened the day-light, it seemed, if possible, more calm than before, not a breath stirred. The sea had not a ripple upon it, and looked like a sheet of silver. The sails hung loosely against the masts, the pendant drooped from the truck perpendicularly downwards, the loose cordage hung motionless; it seemed as though the ocean were a great plain, and the vessel grew out of it. Albert was leaning over the taffrail, thinking of Aylmine, when he heard a voice behind mention his name, and felt a hand upon his shoulder, which seemed to send a bolt of ice through his frame. He turned to see who had intruded upon his thoughts, and found Paul Sachs at his elbow ; he shuddered involuntarily as the man's form met his gaze.

" Here is something to surprise you, unless you expect it," said Sachs, with a sneer.

" What mean you ?" asked Albert.

The pilot answered by pointing over the starboard-bow. Albert turned his eyes in the direction in which he pointed, and saw at a distance a vessel bearing towards them. What was most extraordinary she appeared labouring under a stress of weather; she had scarce a stitch of canvas set, the top-gallant sails were furled, the topsails, mainsails, and foresail, close reefed ; a storm sail, and a try sail aft, was all that was shown to the wind. Although the sea all round appeared as smooth as glass, yet the strange vessel plunged and pitched as though in a sea that was running high. Albert could scarce credit his eyesight, and gazed on it with an earnestness which its extraordinary appearance gave rise to. The Captain came on deck, and his attention was quickly caught by the groups of seamen, and turned om them to the approaching vessel, which still bore on, plunging madly, as though under the influence of a heavy gale.

"My God!" he exclaimed, "what can be the meaning of this?"

No answer was returned, and the strange vessel neared them rapidly, and kept on as though she was standing direct for their vessel. A dead silence reigned on board the Johannes, and an anxious watch was kept on the mysterious stranger. As they got quite close together the strange ship wore, and as she fell off on the other tack, they saw plainly the people on board, heard the hoarse command given in a tone of anxiety through a speaking trumpet, and saw the hurried actions of the seamen obeying them, which an appearance of danger would produce. She shot by them; the wind seemed roaring through the cordage, the masts sprung like pieces of steel, the spray dashed up from the bows in sheets of foam, and in a few minutes she was gone, in as sudden and inexplicable a manner as she had appeared.

"Who, and what can it be?" asked Albert, aloud and unconsciously.

"Who should it be," shouted Paul Sachs, in his ear, "but the Phantom Ship? THE FLYING DUTCHMAN!! Mynheer Vanderdecken."

CHAPTER IX.

THE STORM.—THE WRECK.

ALBERT started, and felt every nerve thrill as he heard the strange vision denominated, and he gazed on the spot where it had disappeared intensely, almost with an expectation of seeing it; but the sky, which a moment before had been clear and bright, was now pervaded with a deep gloom, which rendered everything invisible within twenty yards of the ship. He turned to the spot where Paul Sachs had stood, and, notwithstanding the repugnance which he felt at speaking to him, he determined to question him respecting it, as he appeared to know so much concerning the mystery; but he found him talking to the captain, and saw him point to himself, and the captain following with his eyes the direction in which he pointed. Albert grew confused beneath their glances, and felt as though he stood like a felon, or one who had committed some grievous crime, and they the judges before whom he stood convicted. He was conscious he had done nothing for which he had a right to feel ashamed, yet he seemed to stand as though he had: but a moment's thought restored him to himself, and drawing himself proudly up, he walked towards them. As he approached Paul Sachs left the captain and went forward, and the captain advanced to meet him.

"The pilot has warned me of weather, Mynheer Vanderdecken," he said, as he met Alber.

"Indeed!" said Albert; "I should scarce have thought it; there is no appearance of it."

"That's what I say," retorted the captain; "but th pilot tells me that the appearance of the Phantom Ship is a sure prognosticator of foul weather, or at least some mishap to the vessel which has the ill luck to fall in with her. The name of her commander was Vanderdecken, and the fool pointed to you, and said there was always ill luck in the name."

Albert could not answer, but smiled faintly; and the captain continued—

"As to foul weather, there is little sign of that; this sudden fog is clearing off, and the morn is shining clear enough. Ah, no bad weather to-night."

Albert turned his head and looked around the horizon, and then to the vane at the mast-head.

"The wind has changed," he said.

"Changed!" echoed the captain, hastily; "by Heaven, so it has; we must look to this."

He had scarcely made the remark when long, thin sheets of grey clouds came sweeping up. But a moment before the vessel was rolling in the long swell of the calm sea; the canvas, of which every available stitch was set, hung still and motionless from the yards and spars; not a breath was stirring. Now a ripple was heard at the bow of the vessel, as if there was some slight way upon her; the sails began to flap, and a slight wind from the South-west blew upon their faces. Directly the captain felt this, he ordered the top-gallant and top-sails to be struck; and in another minute the men were scrambling up the rigging and laying out on the yards, executing his orders: ere they had completed their task the wind came rushing along, and when it reached the ship she bowed down before it, and then rose again, throwing the water on each side of her bows as she made way through the water. The wind increased with frightful force; the sails were reduced until there was but a stay-sail forward left, and the vessel flew along as if under a heavy press of canvass.

"This is like magic," said the captain, to Albert. "I feel strangely heavy about the heart," he continued, wiping the perspiration from his forehead. "I do not like this sudden and extraordinary change. It is scarce five minutes since the topsails were hanging in the clue-lines, without a ruffle in the cloth, and now we are scudding furiously under bare poles, with a gale which seems increasing to a hurricane."

The sky was now completely covered with a dense mass of clouds; a darkness which the time of the year did not warrant reigned around; it was impossible to see ten yards from the bow of the ship. The wind roared furiously, the cordage rattled and whistled, the masts bent like whalebone, and the vessel flew along. Albert and the first mate took charge of the helm, and the captain stood at the binnacle, directing them how to steer. The rain poured down in torrents, and the wind blew it with such fury that it was impossible to face it; all the men forward not actually occupied, were sheltering themselves under the bulwarks. Violent as the gale was, the Johannes had as yet behaved uncommonly well; it had not shipped a sea, and danced over the waves like a duck. Long flashes of lightning, accompanied by heavy peals of thunder, now succeded ; the wind increased from roaring to howling frightfully, and suddenly a report like that of a twenty-four pounder was heard, and a white mass flew past them in the air.

"There goes the forestay-sail !" cried the captain. The words had scarcely quitted his lips, when the vessel yawing with the sudden loss of the staysail, shipped a huge sea on the quarter, burying everything near, and sweeping Albert and the first mate from the wheel ; in another minute the ship broached to, a tremendous crash was heard, and the mainmast was carried away. When Albert recovered himself everything was in confusion, but he heard the voice of the captain rising almost supernaturally clear above the storm, giving directions for cutting away the wreck of the fallen mast ; this was soon done, and, relieved by the weight of it, the vessel rode more lightly over the mountainous waves. Two steady seamen had been placed at the wheel, and Albert discovered that the first mate had been washed overboard. The men, half-terrified by the fierceness of the storm, and their feelings influenced by the singular suddenness with which it had arisen, were gathering in knots on the forecastle, and were being worked upon by Paul Sachs, who, from some vindictive motive, was persuading them that Albert's presence was the cause of this violent storm, which would not abate while he was in the vessel, and that they might thank him for it if they were cast away. One man proposed giving him the fate of Jonas. Paul Sachs clapped his hands and laughed, and the rest echoed the sentiment with a cheer ; and, led on by Paul, came aft in a body to put their intention into execution. As they sprung up the poop-ladder, the captain met them, and demanded the cause of this sudden mutinous proceeding.

"Not mutinous, Sir," cried Paul, who was spokesman ; "but I told you that all of the name of Vanderdecken bore ill luck with 'em, wherever they went. Mynheer Vanderdecken, here, has brought this gale about our ears, after our just escaping the breakers, and we mean to clear the ship of him ;" and beckoning his fellows, he proceeded to the binnacle, where Albert was standing, barely recovered from the violent blow he had received in being thrown against the bulwarks by the sea they had shipped ; but throwing himself before them, the captain shouted in a loud and peremptory voice—

"Hold !"

The men stopped instantly from an habitual feeling of obeying the captain's voice.

"Are you mad," he cried, "in an hour like this to attempt a murder? Are you fools," he asked, scornfully, "to let yourselves be persuaded by a malignant wretch, that the presence of an unoffending young man is the cause of what it is the Almighty's pleasure we are labouring under now ! For shame ! Return to your duty at once. And for you, Paul Sachs, if I see a further attempt to excite by lies and cowardice any disaffection among the people, I'll order your into irons immediately. Away with you."

"If you have the courage of rats, and wish to save your lives, you will not be thrust aside from ridding yourselves of a doomed man, who will sink every ship he treads on. Come on !" shouted Paul Sachs.

" Stand back!" roared the captain, drawing his sword, and placing himself in an attitude of defence. Albert, who had heard all that had passed, seized a capstan bar that lay near him, and came to the side of the captain, prepared to sell his life dearly.

" Down with him !" yelled the pilot.

" Down with him !" echoed the men, and rushed on. Ere a blow was struck, the flash and report of a gun was seen and heard near them. A long, fearful, vivid flash of lightning which showed the sea raging terribly, also discovered a vessel with every stitch of canvas set, main-sails, topsails, topgallant-sails, royals, jibs, stay-sails, studding-sails and all, coming furiously, head to wind. Although the moment preceding the lightning it had been pitch dark, a pale light now shed its rays over the sea, showing the coming vessel plainly, and everything on board of her. As she neared them, coming within a few yards, she was observed to wear, and showing her broadside, the captain of her was seen on the deck looking earnestly at the Johannes. Albert, in an instant, with a tumultuous beating at the heart, recognised in him the original of the portrait he had found in the closed chamber.

" The Flying Dutchman!" screamed Paul Sachs, springing to the taffrail.

" MY FATHER ! ! !" exclaimed Albert, mentally, and staggering, fell insensible on the deck.

" I'll have my revenge on you through him," shouted Paul, to the Phantom captain, pointing to the spot where Albert had stood.

" Not this time," answered a clear but melancholy voice. " It is not to be."

" It shall ! it shall !" yelled the pilot, in his energy jumping with his knees upon the taffrail, and shaking his fist at the Phantom. The spectre smiled, and the Johannes falling in the trough of the sea, gave a lurch, which pitched the pilot into the foaming waters. A loud scream, followed by a scornful laugh, was all that was heard ; and the Phantom Ship faded away from their astonished sight.

When Albert recovered, he found sufficient to create the greatest alarm ; he knew not how long he had remained senseless, but there was no one at the helm ; it was lashed amid ships. The captain was nowhere to be seen, and the crew were forward, drinking, carousing, singing, and dancing, acting like mad devils, instead of men upon the brink of death. He hesitated whether he should proceed forward, but thinking that his presence might only exasperate these madmen, and feeling sick at heart, he descended the poop-ladder, and entered the cabin. There he saw poor little Von Schmidt, the supercargo, in his shirt, seated on the edge of his berth, looking as wretchedly frightened and miserable as it was possible for man to look. The captain was nowhere to be seen, and Albert turned to quit the cabin. He was in no mood to speak to the little man ; but as he was passing through the door, he heard the voice of Von Schmidt calling him back.

" Stay ! stay! Mynheer, don't leave me here, all alone. Oh, I shall die ! be drowned ! Lord have mercy upon me!"

Albert turned back and told him to dress himself and come upon deck with him, for it was, in the present state of affairs, dangerous to stay in the cabin.

" But the bear, Mynheer ! the bear ! I can't come," cried the little man. Albert looked, and found that the bear had placed himself beneath the supercargo's berth, and was sleeping comfortably enough.

" He is harmless ; he will not touch you," replied Albert ; " be quick, there is no time to lose ;" and he assisted the man down, and hurriedly helped him to dress. They went on deck, and ere Albert had reached the top of the poop-ladder, he felt the vessel run on a sand-bank, and swing round broadside to the sea. He sprung to the windward bulwark and clung to it. Little Schmidt was thrown by the shock off the ladder, and he immediately scrambled into the cabin, falling over the bear, which was disturbed, and making his way out. The sea now made heavy breaches over the vessel, the masts went by the board, and in an incredibly short space of time the Johannes became an entire and complete wreck. Those of the crew who were not lost by falling to leeward through intoxication, and being drowned, seized on the boat on the booms. They cut away the lashing, and waited for a sea : it came, a tremendous one, and lifted the boat from the chocks to the quarter. Luckily one of the men had made the painter fast, or the sea, which was a very huge one, would have swept the boat away entirely. However, they all succeded in getting into it but Albert, who, when he approached it with that intention, was instantly thrust back, and ere he could remonstrate with them there was a cry that a sea was coming, and he was compelled for his own safety to leave the boat and cling to the bulwarks, getting under their lee, to prevent himself being washed overboard. The sea came and bore them, men and boat, away ; he saw them on the summit of a mountainous wave, and then they were carried beyond his sight. The vessel had been urged by the violence of the waves high upon the sand bank, and Albert found after a short time that the wind was dropping—the tide receding, and that every sea came with less and less violence over the wreck. The morning was now breaking ; as it grew lighter he saw the land was about a quarter of a mile distant, that it appeared to be a high sterile mountain, but he could not conjecture in the most remote degree where he was. He discovered that the jolly-boat was still left and unhurt, and as this presented a good means of escape, he set about fitting it with spars and sails. The weather had now moderated, and as the sun rose it became quite calm and smooth. Albert, although wearied and exhausted by the incidents of the night, worked hard to get all ready, and proceeded to the store room, where he found plenty of provisions. He laid up a good store of biscuit, beef, and rum ; and thinking that he might have an opportunity of saving some valuables, he entered the cabin. Here he found Von Schmidt in his berth, which, luckily for him, happened to be on the at present elevated side of the vessel, groaning faintly. He went up to him and spoke to him. The little man opened his eyes and stared, without scarce knowing who and what he stared at; but Albert, pleased at finding him alive and at the prospect of a companion, even though he was such a miserable little dog, spoke cheerfully to him, and helped him out of his berth. He could not on doing so repress his laughter, when he discovered that the bear was comfortably domiciled with him.

" Why, how's this ?" asked Albert, "how did you manage to get bruin in your bed ?"

" Oh," returned Schmidt, in a weak voice, " the horrid monster! when I heard that dreadful noise, and was thrown down that dreadful height, I scrambled in a dreadful fright into the cabin, and fell over that dreadful wretch ; when I got up, dreadfully alarmed, I jumped up into my bed, for I found the water coming in. Imagine my dreadful situation when I found that dreadful brute followed me, climbed up, and actually got into my very bed. I thought I must have died with horror, and expected every instant to be swallowed up."

" But he did not hurt you," said Albert, amused at his dreadful account.

" Why, no !" said the little man, instinctively, feeling himself all over, " but he made me very warm."

" Possibly," returned Albert, who could allow for the perspiration the supercargo's fears must have created. He then related to him how matters stood, their chance of escape, and requested his assistance and co-operation for their mutual safety. To this of course Schmidt assented, and going upon deck, after taking everything which might be of value if they escaped, they proceeded to get the boat afloat. This cost them more labour than they expected, but as ' true hope ne'er tires,' they persevered, and their exertions were at length crowned with success; they got safely in and hoisting a sail, with a light breeze they stood out to sea. Albert determined to keep a good offing, but not lose the land. All that day and the next night they were sailing, taking it in turn to sleep. Albert, when his turn for rest came, gave copious directions to Von Schmidt how to act, which his fears made him scrupulously fulfil. For three days they sailed without meeting with anything which could create a hope of rescue in them. As Albert steered during the night, he slept in the morning, and on the morning of the fourth day Schmidt awoke him, and pointing to an object, asked Albert if it was not a ship. Albert joyfully pronounced it to be one, and putting the head of the boat direct for it, and having a favourable wind, giving up the helm to Schmidt, and telling him how to steer, he hoisted everything which would hold a little wind ; and was delighted to find that they made capital headway. He had brought some fire-arms and ammunition with him from the ship, in case he might want them, if he unfortunately fell in with some inhospitable natives of the coast, of whom he had heard sad accounts. As the boat flew over the water, they strained their eyes anxiously to discover if they were observed by the persons on board the ship they were endeavouring to overtake, but the vessel still held on her course. Albert found with pleasure that he was gaining fast upon them; the masts and hull were now plainly visible, and after three or four hours of eager excitement, there was not the distance of three miles between them. Albert now fired a gun, and as the smoke cleared away looked out for a returning signal ; but no— he saw no symptom that they were seen, and proceeded to reload his piece.

" They seem to be altering their sails," said Schmidt.

" What ?" asked Albert, raising his head.

Surprise and horror of Aylmine on discovering the dead body of Winken Kroots.

"Why, they are firing at us! Oh, let us go back," cried Schmidt, in alarm.

"Hurrah!" shouted Albert, "they are backing their topsails and lying-to."

This was the case; in half-an-hour Albert and Schmidt were safely on board one of the Company's ships, returning home from a successful voyage. Albert related to the captain the principal circumstances of his disastrous voyage, keeping to himself those which related to his own peculiar destiny. A quick passage brought them again to Holland, and Albert once more found himself in Amsterdam.

CHAPTER X.

SHOWS HOW MUCH WINKEN KROOTS LOVED GOLD.

ALBERT felt uncertain how to act respecting his return to his wife. He had arrived at Amsterdam some months before she could possibly expect

No. 10. L

him. He had no friend to whom he could entrust the delicate task of breaking his sudden return to her, and he feared coming upon her too abruptly. His anxiety was great to see her, and he approached the street in which his house stood without yet coming to any determination. He stood opposite the house, and still he could not form a plan. At length a man in the garb of a seaman passed, and Albert, as he came up, recognised in him the first mate of the vessel which had rescued him. He hailed him and said—

" You remember me ?"

" Surely," replied the man ; " Mynheer Vanderdecken, whom we picked up at sea ?"

" The same," returned Albert. " You will oblige me if you will execute a mission for me. Having, through being wrecked as you know, returned so many months before I am expected, I fear coming too suddenly before my wife ; knowing her strong feelings, I am fearful that a sudden revolution might be fatal to her. Will you be good enough to knock, and say that you bring good news—that you expect me home soon, and, in fact, break my arrival to her as well as you can."

" I'll do my best, Sir," said the man ; " but I am not used to these little delicate tasks, and am almost afraid I shall not acquit myself so well as I could wish ; but I will try."

Albert thanked him, and stood on one side while he knocked at the door. In a short space of time it was opened by Winken Kroots.

" Is Madam Vanderdecken within ?" asked the mate.

" What do you want to know for ?" inquired Kroots.

" I wish to see her," said the mate.

" What do you wish to see her for ?" asked Winken.

" That I will tell her when I see her," said the mate.

" And why not to me ?" cried Winken.

" If you will tell her that it is a person from Mynheer Vanderdecken ——"

Ere he could say another word, Aylmine, who had heard part of the foregoing conversation, was by his side.

" You have brought intelligence from my husband ?" she exclaimed, in an agony of impatience. " He is alive ? well ? happy ?—Speak, for Heaven's sake ! I feel as if my heart would burst ! "

" He is alive, well, and I believe happy ;" returned the mate. " He will be with you much sooner than you could possibly expect."

" How looked he ? what said he ? where is he ? when shall I see him ?" were asked by Aylmine in a breath.

" He was wrecked, but was saved. He looks, I believe, well. He said he should very shortly see you. He is not a week's journey from here; and I have no doubt you will see him in less time than I have mentioned," said the mate, replying to every question.

" Coming home so soon ?" observed Winken ; " and wrecked ? Why he must have lost all his guilders, and will want more ? Suppose we move away, Aylmine, and let nobody know where we have gone ; then all the guilders and plate that remains will be ours so easily."

The mate stared, and Aylmine silenced Winken by a look.

" Is he far from here now, think you ?"

" Can you bear sudden meetings—surprises ?" asked the mate.

" He is here, he is near me, I know. Tell me, I beseech you ; do not fear my weakness. I know he is here. Albert ! Albert !" cried Aylmine, with intense excitement, and sprung through the doorway. In another minute she was buried in his arms—she tried to speak—laughed hysterically, and fainted dead away. They bore her into the cottage, and it was not long ere they restored her to consciousness. She gazed on Albert, as he held her in his arms, with all the fondness and tenderness which eyes can express, and smiled through her tears, as she told him that she cared little for the circumstances which had caused his return. He had returned to her alive and well, and that was all and everything to her. The mate was warmly thanked for the able and delicate manner in which he had acquitted himself, and with a recompense, which was bestowed in a manner that could not hurt his pride in the smallest degree, he departed, with invitations to visit, and expressions of friendliness.

Winken endeavoured to look pleased, but his inability was too apparent : it is difficult to express one feeling, and be tortured and worked up by another—its complete opposite.

" We are glad you have come home," he said ; " when do you go again ?"

Albert stared for a moment, and then laughed. "Oh, soon, I dare say," he exclaimed.

" Do not talk about it," observed Aylmine ; " you are scarcely returned."

" Your guilders are all safe, will you count them ?" cried Winken. Aylmine, will you give Mynheer Vanderdecken the keys ? He would like, I am sure, to know that his money is all safe—I will help you count them."

" I am much obliged to you," returned Albert, amused at Winken's incessant recurrence to the guilders ; " but I am quite satisfied with regard to their safety. They seem to have given you an infinitude of trouble, and when I depart on my next voyage," he continued, looking at Aylmine with a smile, " I shall take them with me."

" Oh, no, no, no, no," cried Winken, hurriedly, "you cannot do that; you must not do that."

" Why not ?" asked Albert, who felt pleased at teazing the little miser.

" You have been wrecked—lost everything ; you would do the same if you took your money. Oh, no, you must not take your money !" said Winken with nervous anxiety.

" You are mistaken," remarked Albert. " It is true I have been wrecked, but I have saved so many things of value to the Company, that I have returned the possessor of a larger sum than I took with me."

Here the conversation dropped, but when Albert and Aylmine were alone, he inquired if she had been troubled by Winken's thirst for the money. She replied in the affirmative, and said that he was for ever in the room containing it, feasting his eyes upon the plate, and trying every artifice he was master of to obtain the keys from her; but, being aware of the absence of all principle in him, she had exercised her utmost caution and vigilance in keeping them in her own possession.

Two months passed away, and Albert enjoyed the most perfect happiness, if the alloy of his father's doom, and his own duty to alleviate it, producing from its mysterious nature incertitude, be excepted. His voyage had as yet only satisfied him that there really was a Phantom Ship; and from the transient glance he had of its captain, he felt almost assured that it must be his father : yet his mind might have been so worked upon by previous reflections and occurrences that he might have made a likeness where none really existed ; and the ship appeared to others as well as to himself ; indeed he had had no sign of recognition from the mysterious phantom, and he doubted whether it was actually necessary for him to proceed with his intention of carrying out his oath. He reasoned, speculated, and worked himself up to the same state of doubt as he had laboured under ere he first departed. One day he had thought more intensely than usual upon the subject, and at night, complaining of being unwell, he retired early to rest. In the morning he awoke in a fever, and Winken prescribed for him. Aylmine was alarmed, and tended Albert with the fondest care and anxiety ; every little thought that could produce aught to contribute to his comfort and return to health was called into action by her. Every symptom was attended and scrutinised by her, and every dose administered by Winken was questioned, and its qualities made known to her ere it was given. In three days Albert began to recover fast, and she mentioned it with delight to Winken, who grinned with a singular expression when he heard it. She noticed it, and a strange feeling of distrust and alarm crept over her. Albert had been delirious, and once during it had laughed long and loudly, and said, "I will take all my gold and plate away from you, Winken Kroots, when I depart on my next voyage, and that will be very soon. I will not leave a guilder or a piece of plate behind, Winken—No—no," and then he burst into a violent fit of laughter. Winken was in the room at the time, and Aylmine had noticed that since that hour he had been restless, and moved about muttering, as if he had himself been delirious ; that he had been in the room where the plate was kept more constantly than ever, and now this grin, cold, and conveying a sinister expression, quite startled her. " Surely," she thought, " he cannot be so abandoned to all feeling of humanity as to attempt to poison him. The Almighty preserve me !" she ejaculated, " it cannot be !" Nevertheless, she watched him more closely than ever. The next night, Albert, finding himself unable to sleep, Winken said he would make him up a composing draught, which would prove a pleasing incentive to slumber.

" You will sleep sound enough, I'll warrant me," he continued, " and without dreaming too. Ha! ha! without dreaming. Ho! ho! ho!"

There was something peculiarly harsh and grating in his laugh when he said this, and Aylmine determined that, whatever the draught might be, Albert should not take it. She therefore made some warm wine-and-water, and put a few drops of opium in it. As she was about to give it to Albert, Winken entered with the draught, and told Aylmine to administer it, and at the same time inquired what it was she was about giving Albert in the cup. She said "some warm wine-and-water." He told her not to give it him, but to give the draught he had brought in with him, and he held it to her. His hand trembled she perceived as he gave it; and, more resolved than ever, she turned to the bed and dexterously changed the cups ; returning the same cup with the mixture to Winken which he had brought in with him, and giving the wine-and-water which she had mixed to Albert. Winken went hastily away, and Albert drank the wine. He soon fell into a gentle slumber. Aylmine watched by him unwearyingly all night, occasionally kissing his forehead and lips, wiping the perspiration from his brow, and offering up prayers for his recovery and future happiness. In the morning Albert awoke refreshed, and, with the exception of weakness, almost well. The sun was rising high, and as Winken was not stirring Aylmine went to call him. She entered his sleeping apartment, he was not there; she went to the room containing the plate and money, making sure of meeting him there, as usual, glutting his eyes with the sight of the precious metal. What was her horror and surprise to find him seated upright by the beaufet, his eyes extended wide open, his hand clutching at the chest belonging to Albert, the door of the beaufet having been forced open by him. His jaw had fallen and he was quite dead. The cause was soon explained : upon the table stood the cup emptied of the contents he had intended for Albert, in the hope of obtaining his gold. The little wretch had mixed a deadly poison, and had himself fallen a victim to his own villany. The whole circumstances flashed upon the mind of Aylmine at once, and her loud scream fell upon the ear of Albert, who, in a state of excitement, hastily attired himself, and, seeking the room from whence the sound had proceeded, found Winken Kroots as we have described, dead; and Aylmine fainting on the floor.

CHAPTER XI.

ALBERT RECEIVES A SIGN.—HIS SECOND VOYAGE.

HE raised her, and bearing her in his arms to a seat, used every means to restore her to consciousness, and after a short time succeeded ; but the exertion in his weak condition was too much for him, and he was glad to regain the bed which he had so hastily quitted.

A few days' quiet and care restored him to his pristine health. Winken Kroots was laid in his grave, and Albert and Aylmine were left quite alone in the world. They had sought no acquaintances; they had not required them, and therefore had not made them. The only relative Albert had possessed was his mother's brother, and he had died lately, leaving property to a large amount to Albert. On Aylmine's side, her parents were both dead ; and having been brought an infant from the East, whatever relatives might have belonged to her she could not know —they were dead to her, or as if they had never existed. Thus they were alone, loving and loved—all in all—the whole world to each other. Time passed away, and the strong feeling which had urged Albert to fulfil the oath he had made was softened to a considerable extent, and he began to doubt whether there would be any possibility of ever succeeding in his task, and ultimately to doubt whether he had not been labouring under a diseased imagination. Certain it was that the charm of Aylmine's society was fast obliterating every other feeling but that of the pleasure of being with her. Day succeeded day, week followed week, and still found him contentedly at home with Aylmine. As the thought occasionally arose within him that his supineness in his father's fate was blameable, he dismissed it as an intruder, although he had an inward conviction that, delay it as he might, he must fulfil his task. Twelve months had elapsed since he returned from his first voyage, when one morning he received a notice from the Company that an eligible opportunity offered, if he had a desire to purchase shares. As this was an intention he had cherished since his first outset in search of his father, he immediately attended to the notice, and became a purchaser to a large amount, with a promise of the command of a ship when a vacancy occurred. This circumstance aroused him for a short time from his lethargy, and he conceived the idea of a voyage with a feeling of interest; but there was also a feeling which acted as a check upon his impatience to commence it. He had himself twice seen the Phantom Ship—each time it had brought disaster with it. Every narration that he had heard respecting it had involved accounts of disasters, shipwrecks, and death. It had never appeared to the crew of a vessel but it was the forerunner of a terrible fate for them; and on this account Albert felt a hesitation to risk the lives of men who would have no interest in the object for which he prosecuted his dangerous task. " Still," thought he, " this vessel has appeared to many—I know not how many—with whom I have been in no way concerned; it has brought misfortune upon them without my having been in the vessel. I have not been the cause; besides, I have yet to be satisfied that I am so immediately connected with the mystery as I have hitherto firmly believed myself to be. It has appeared to others as well as to me. It betokened danger to them equally as it did when I saw it. There was no difference in its results when I met with it, to what there has ever been when others have fallen in with it. My presence had no influence upon it; although my imagination, overheated by former occurrences, made it have a strong influence upon me. My mother's story was a singular and a fearful one; the circumstances which I encountered after her death were also of a strange and unaccountable nature. There must be a species of truth in it all—it could not be the result of strong fancies, and if it is all true. I must go on with it—must prosecute it, until I have succeeded in my task or perish in the attempt, and if I involve in my undertaking the lives of others, why should I feel a hesitation to do so? We are all under the protection of an Almighty Providence, which will not suffer the destruction of a human being without a motive in which its influence appears; and do not men for a miserable stipend risk their lives daily for the intrigues and cabals of parties stirring up war between nations on the wretchedest trifles imaginable? Why, then, should I hesitate to command a ship and proceed with the fulfilment of my oath?—And yet, why should I quit a happy home—a being whom I love beyond anything this world can bestow—on a task of uncertainty, doubt, difficulty, and danger? Assist me, Holy Mother, for I am torn by conflicting passions!"

Thus did Albert reflect one night as he lay by the side of Aylmine, agitated by doubts and desires as to what line he should pursue. It was a clear moonlight night, and the rays of the moon came brightly into the room, showing some parts of it as clearly as though daylight was shining in, while other parts were quite dark. Albert was gazing on the moonlight, and gradually felt a sensation of cold and awe creep over him, as he became conscious of a figure standing where, the moment previous, he had been gazing on vacancy. Aylmine was sleeping by his side. He had not heard the door of the apartment unclose, he had not turned his eyes from the spot, nor had he seen the figure, which he was now looking fearfully upon, move to the spot on which it stood. The effect was as if a mist had cleared off and discovered the figure standing there. He was so taken by surprise that he had neither power to move or speak, while he felt all about his heart as cold as ice. He kept his eyes fixed upon it—it was motionless. He essayed to speak, but his tongue clave to the roof of his mouth, as the features of his mother became distinctly visible in those of the mysterious stranger, and he knew the spirit of his mother stood before him.

"Albert!" said a faint, sweet voice, but, oh! the tones came so well known upon his ears.

"Mother!" burst from his lips with fervency.

The figure waved its hand in a quiet yet dignified manner, as if to command silence, and then spoke in a voice which came to Albert as an old melody breaks on our ears which we heard when we were happy and lost for years, hearing it again at some remote and unexpected period.

"Albert," she said, "in the hour which I was taken from the earth I related to thee the cause of my unceasing melancholy. I told thee everything which I was mistress of respecting the unhappy fate of thy father. When I had completed my tale, it pleased the Heavenly Father to take me to his bosom, and thou hadst circumstances and things placed before thee rarely exhibited to mortals, to convince thee that truth had been spoken. Thou readst a letter, addressed to thee, which was found by thee in a room which had remained unopened eighteen years. The letter was taken from thee immediately thou had'st been made acquainted with its contents. An oath was made by thee—and registered, Albert. Thou didst proceed on thy first voyage, and saw thy father; in that, also, wert thou satisfied that there was such a being, labouring under such circumstances as had been narrated to thee. Thou thyself distinguished in the captain of that Spectre Ship thine own features, and that he was the original of the portrait now hanging in the chamber beneath this; yet dost thou doubt, after all these signs have been given thee, that thou shouldst proceed in the fulfilling a registered oath to avert thy father's doom, being the only instrument by which it can be effected. Let thy doubts pass from thee; everything is as thou hast been told and shown. Let not its mystery confound thee. Believe, and act upon thy belief. The Almighty power which considers the welfare of the smallest created thing in nature will not forget thee. Be firm—be resolute, and thou shalt succeed. And now, dear Albert, child of my soul! let me tell thee, ere we part never to meet again until thy soul shall have quitted its earthly tenement, how fondly, how dearly I have cherished the remembrance of thy conduct to me. From the time thy father quitted me until I ceased to exist on the earth, thou wert the stay, the solace, the only tie that kept me to existence. Thy childhood was one sum of love, of devotion to me. As thou grew up, all thy father's impetuosity of character was inherited by thee, but tempered by they tenderness of feeling to me, thy mother. Never didst thou, dear Albert, give me one moment's pain or uneasiness. Thou wert intuitively noble in thy character, as thou wert amiable and gentle in disposition. The memory of thy goodness is on my soul unsullied, and believe me, my dearest son, thy difficulties and dangers in this world will be rewarded tenfold in that which is to come. Farewell! bless thee, my dear child! Farewell! Remember thy oath!"

The voice died away, and Albert was gazing on vacancy as before. The blood, which seemed to have left his frame, rushed back violently to his heart; he groaned heavily and fainted away. When he recovered, Aylmine was leaning over him weeping, and bathing his temples. She awoke instantly he had groaned, and became dreadfully alarmed at finding her repeated inquiries were unanswered, and Albert lying senseless. When he was so far recovered as to be able to speak, he told her what had occurred, and that now, in spite of every circumstance, he would depart on his mission, to accomplish his father's release. Aylmine bowed her head meekly, and placing her hands on his, told him she would acquiesce in whatever he though right without a word to turn him from it, however pained she might be by its results.

"The same gentle kindness ever, beloved Aylmine," said Albert, as he embraced her.

The morning sun rose and found Albert dressed and ready to depart to the Company's offices to inquire respecting a ship. Ere he quitted the house, a violent knock came at the door; it was opened, and in walked Paul Sachs. Albert started as he encountered this man, and stared at him with astonishment. He had fully believed that he was drowned when the boat and crew had disappeared, apparently overwhelmed by that huge wave, on the summit of which Albert had seen them, when they were borne from the wreck of the Johannes.

"I thought you were dead," said Albert, half shrinking back, more from an idea that there was something unearthly in the man, than from any fear his presence had created.

"You were mistaken, then," replied he; "you see I am not."

"I thought you were drowned; it seemed impossible for any boat to live in such a surf as was running at that moment," exclaimed Albert.

"You escaped," said Paul with a grin.

"True," replied he.

"Do you suppose you were the only favoured one in the ship's company?" asked the pilot with a sneer.

Paul Sachs pronounces the doom of Vanderdecken.

" No," replied Albert, coldly, an inclination rising within him to expel Paul Sachs from his presence ; " but the circumstances in which we were placed were different. You went away in a small vessel in the night, during a heavy surf ; I waited till the tide was down, the wind abated, and daylight to assist me. It was more probable for me to save my life than you ; that is the only reason I have for surprise that you should be alive."

" The supercargo escaped with you ?" said the pilot.

" He did," answered Albert.

" Oh," grinned the fellow, " then you and I are the only two left of that expedition ; the little officer lost his life in consequence of being in too great a hurry to show off his importance lately. He was appointed to a new vessel, and in ascending the ship's side, he began his strut too soon, missed his footing, and fell overboard. He was drawn under the vessel, and drowned before it was scarcely know what had become of him. The ship's company were thus rid of an upstart, little wretch; and the Company lost a servant whose own interest was of far more importance to him than the interests of any employers could be, Company or no Company;" and Paul Sachs gave a long laugh of apparently great satisfaction.

No. 11. M

Albert eyed him with a feeling of excessive disgust, at the same time feeling sorry to hear of the death of his companion, who was sociable and agreeable enough when his danger put his consequence out of countenance.

"What is your business with me?" asked Albert abruptly.

"You are right," sneered Sachs, "it is business, I should not come to you on pleasure. I have been sent by the Company; here is a packet for you; I believe it contains an appointment for you to a ship in which I sail as pilot."

"You?" cried Albert, with mortification mingled with astonishment.

"Yes," returned the pilot; "but not as Paul Sachs. I take my own name this time. You will remember it when I tell you, Mynheer Vanderdecken; it is *Peter* Graat, once chief mate to the Amstelredamme." Saying this, and placing the packet in Albert's hand, he passed out of the house.

Albert clasped his hands to his forehead, and exclaimed—

"This then is the sign. I have seen my mother's spirit, and he who pronounced my father's doom hath been with me on my search, hath each time brought me the notice to depart, and is a second time to sail with me on my extraordinary mission. His fate is interwoven with mine, of that I am assured. Well, be it so! The will of Heaven be done!"

He opened the packet and found he had been appointed to the command of an entirely new ship, named the Amsterdammer. The name excited an emotion in the breast of Albert; it was the same name with a slight corruption, as the vessel his father was beating about in.

"It is a strange coincidence," he remarked; "but it all apparently tends to one point. Something tells me I shall be successful this time; but what the results may be as regards myself is all hidden in darkness from me; every effort I make to think upon it I find futile.

A week was allowed him to prepare to go on board, the ship sailing at the termination of that time if the wind served. Albert proceeded to get everything necessary, and met with the co-operation and assistance of Aylmine, who attended to his slightest wish, whose love made her possess every forethought which even in the minutest trifles could contribute to his happiness. She ever showed the most earnest desire to add to it in every way it was possible; and in word, thought, and action, she was to him the most fond, doting lover, as she was an affectionate wife. As the day drew nearer for their coming separation, her brow grew sadder, and often in their converse would she turn her head to conceal the large tears, which, in spite of every effort, would force themselves into her eyes. Albert tried everything in his power to soothe and comfort her, and his efforts only seemed to add to her grief. He begged of her to think of some way in which she could be made more comfortable or happy during his absence; but she burst into a torrent of tears, and exclaimed—

"I cannot, dear Albert, be happy, while you are away from me; there is nothing that can compensate for your absence. I shall be alone, with only the recollection of you to cheer me, while the uncertainty of your fate will rack and tear my soul almost to madness. I know I ought not to say this—that it is unkindness to say such words on the eve of your departure ; but, dear Albert, I have striven against it in vain—I have tried to keep it, but I cannot. There is but one way to afford me consolation for the danger of the undertaking you are entering upon—that is, to let me go with you. I acknowledge, if you cannot consent to it with honour as regards your arrangements with the Company, I will submit to my fate unrepiningly ; but, oh, Albert ! do not leave me behind if you can prevent it. Think of the anguish that I must endure, alone, in this place, watching wearyingly, unceasingly, and anxiously, for months—perhaps years—for your return. Think of this; and if you are in dangers, who should share them but she who has devoted her life to you, until death shall part us ?"

Albert, while he acknowledged the affection which dictated the desire, still used every argument to dissuade her from attempting such an undertaking; but she was immovable. If it was possible to take her, she implored him to do so; and the strong wish he had for her to be near him induced him to yield to her wishes, although the prospect of many dangers stared him in the face ; yet his love, over-stepping his judgment, took from him the power of saying nay ; and, therefore, Aylmine prepared herself to accompany him. His house and furniture he left in the care of the Company, with directions, in case of his and his wife's death ere their return, they were to be sold, and the proceeds to be devoted to charitable purposes. He likewise invested his money with the same directions, and upon the day named by the Company he had everything which he purposed taking with him placed on board; and with Aylmine, he was received at the ship's side with all honours, as the captain of the Amsterdammer.

CHAPTER XII.

A STORY CONCERNING THE FLYING DUTCHMAN.

VERY fine weather attended them on the first portion of their journey, and after a slow (but scarcely tedious from the beauty of the weather) journey, the Amsterdammer anchored off Table Bay. It had sailed with the fleet, and had now stopped with them to take in provisions and water. Here a week passed away waiting for a wind; at length a favourable one sprung up. The foretop-bowline was cast loose, the anchor weighed, and the Amsterdammer being all-a-taunt-o, she stood out to sea with ensign and pendant flying.

" She walks through the water prettily, Sir," said the first-mate, touching his hat to Albert.

" Yes," returned Albert, " she travels."

" Ah, Sir," retorted the man, who was the same person that had so well broken the arrival of Albert, from his first voyage, to Aylmine, and whom Albert had appointed chief-mate to the Amsterdammer, knowing, from what he had witnessed on his way home, his admirable capabilities as a seaman. " She is as pretty a bit of craft as ever I trod on blue water."

" We've yet to learn," answered Albert, smiling, " what she will do upon a wind."

" Anything, I'm sure," replied the mate, " that wood and iron can do. I believe there is'nt a duck on a fish-pond to equal her. Why, its my opinion she'd stay under double-reefed topsails alone, against the heaviest sea that ever run; and I never saw but one vessel that did that."

" Ay," said Albert, " and what vessel was that ?"

" The FLYING DUTCHMAN !" returned the mate; " but she's not of this earth, or I might say of this water ; but, be it how it may, I saw her tack under double-reefed topsails—no courses to help her—when the vessel that I was in found her rigging and bare poles hold too much wind.—Ah, it was a gale that night !"

" Where were you when you fell in with her ?" inquired Albert, with an air of interest.

" Homeward bound, North-east of the Cape ; not a great way from where we are now," replied the chief-mate. " It was a strange affair. Should you like to hear it ?"

" Very much," replied Albert; who was just about to ask him to relate all that had transpired when he encountered the Phantom Ship.

" It was on a Friday evening," commenced the mate, clearing his throat for a yarn, " that the affair happened. It had been blowing fresh all day, and as night approached we saw it getting up very black to windward. The to'gaunt-sails were struck, and the top-sails double-reefed, as soon as the brewing gale began to show itself. Wheugh it came rushing along, and we soon found that we were obliged to strike everything, and make all alow and aloft as snug as it could be made; ay, and even then, we run before the wind like mad. ' Sail, a-head !' shouted a man in the tops. I danced forward, and sure enough I saw a vessel, under double-reefed topsails, bearing right down upon us—in the wind's-eye, Captain. It neared us. I shouted to the man at the wheel to port the helm, which he did—hard. It was of no use, they shifted their helm too, but only to bring their head in a line with ours. On they came, and just as we expected them to run right aboard of us, they luffed up, and run alongside. Two or three of their men were on our rigging in an instant, and lashed us together as nimbly and easily as if we were riding on a lake, instead of being on a tremendous sea. We were still running before the wind, and their vessel seemed to have no check upon us. Presently their captain came on board. He looked pale and thin; and, excuse me, Captain Vanderdecken, he was as like you in features as it is possible for one man to be like another ; and, what makes the coincidence more strange, he was of the same name: for he brought out letters, one of which he said was for his dear, dear wife, Estelle Vanderdecken; who resided in Floris Graat, Amsterdam, and was lamenting his absence in grief and despair. I advanced to take his letter, but I was forcibly pulled back by the second-mate, a man who, if I am not mistaken, is pilot in this vessel, but under a different name ?"

"Ha!" cried Albert, and started, while he felt his cheek blanch and his breast heave with anxiety as the mate's narration proceeded. "Pray, what name had he then?" he asked.

"Paul Sachs," replied the mate; "and I'm sure it is him, although he calls himself Peter Graat, now."

"Well, and what of him?" asked Albert, striving to affect an indifference which he could not feel.

"Why, he held me back, and shouted, 'That is the Flying Dutchman, if you take his letters they will sink the ship. When I heard the name I drew back of course, and the captain went round to each, offering them. In the most piteous accents he said, "He had been beating about for years, without being able to gain a port. That since he left Amsterdam, he had received but one letter, which told him that his sweet wife and boy were well, and would be happy but for his absence, and were anxiously waiting his return. This letter he drew from his breast; after kissing it fervently, he showed it to us, and the tears rolled down his pale cheeks, as he found every one shrink from his approach. He clasped his hands, and bowed his head in bitterness of spirit. Our captain, who was as generous-hearted a fellow as ever stepped a ship's plank, affected by what he witnessed, cried out, 'It aint clear to me how a packet of letters can sink a ship, as well-built and as taut as any that ever swam, so give me your letters, Mynheer, and if I reach port before you, I will deliver them. There, now, no thanks, but about ship and sheer off; this is no weather to keep company. The strange captain bowed, placed his letters in our captain's hand, and quitting our vessel was on board his own in a minute. The lashings were cast loose, and we parted company with a bound, as if we had been shot out of a four-and-twenty pounder. We gazed after them, and saw them pitching and tossing furiously, and it was then I saw her tack under double-reefed topsails; the vessel came round like a sloop in fine weather. Well, cried the Captain with a whistle, when he saw her do it, 'if that vessel don't get into port, it aint the fault of the wood and iron about her.' Well, Sir, while he was looking at her she faded from his sight; she did'nt appear to be above a mile from us, it was not so dark but we could see thrice that distance; we lost her, however, and we thought it strange."

"Did any disaster follow the visit of this strange vessel?" inquired Albert, dreading a reply.

"Why, I am coming to that," returned the mate. "When the Flying Dutchman was gone, the Captain placed the letters on the binnacle, with a piece of iron on them to prevent their blowing overboard; but Paul Sachs took them up and cast them over the side, saying 'he would not risk his life for the Captain's weakness.' Lord, what a rage the Captain went in. He ordered the second-mate in irons, and swore he'd take the law in his own hands, and run him up to the yard-arm. However, he cooled on the subject, for, during the night the wind dropped, and when the morning came we were becalmed. During the day we found the vessel had sprung a leak; we could not find out where it was, but we found that it gained on the pumps, though slowly. The pumps were kept hard at work, the men working in gangs; but we found that we could not reduce the leak. Two days passed away, and the men getting dreadfully fatigued, began to murmur. The Captain found that the vessel could not be saved. He had all the boats fitted up, and stored with provisions; a raft was also constructed of all the light spars, fitted with a mast and sails, and made as comfortable as time and materials would allow. Lots were then drawn for the boats and raft, and when everything was completed, the boats and raft were launched, and the people, according to their respective lots, took their berths. The last morning, the men had not worked the pumps, and the leak increased rapidly. We left our vessel, the boats towing the raft, and in about a couple of hours we saw our vessel settle bodily down. Her hull disappeared, she turned over on one side, and down she went. The Captain looked on her to the last, and when her trucks disappeared and left nothing visible where she had been, he buried his face on his knees and wept like a child.

We knocked about for a few days, we were then picked up by a vessel going to the East; they took us on board, and speaking soon after with a vessel homeward-bound, we were put on board and all got safely back to Amsterdam."

"A singular adventure," said Albert, when he had concluded.

"Yes," replied the mate. "Did you ever meet the Flying Dutchman?" he asked.

"Once," replied Albert, turning his head away.

"Oh, indeed! and what took place?" interrogated he.

"Something of the same sort," replied Albert, turning on his heel, and then affected to be busying himself in the ship's progress, to ward off any further inquiries, which he felt he could not answer without embarrassment. "There's a little more strength in the breeze just now; I think it is coming on to blow."

"Shall we take in the topgallant-sails?" asked the mate.

"Ay, ay," said Albert, "take them in, and turn up the hands to reef the topsails; the wind's increasing, and we are getting on too fast already. We've now left the fleet a deuced long way to leeward."

"Ay, ay, Sir," returned the mate, and went forward giving the necessary command, which was promptly obeyed.

Albert having seen that everything was all right, went below to Aylmine. He found her weeping; he folded his arm round her waist, and inquired the cause. For a short time she would not satisfy his request; at length she said that something had transpired which had made her low-spirited. Albert anxiously inquired what it could be. She hesitated, and he begged of her, as she valued his peace of mind, to tell him what had occurred, and not keep him in a suspense which was torture to him.

"Well, Dear Albert," she said, "while you were upon deck, I was engaged in reading a book. I was intent upon the subject, when suddenly I experienced that horrid coldness—that feeling of awe which we may be supposed to endure when a being from the grave stands before us. I shivered, and felt as though I dared not raise my eyes from the book I was reading; and yet I had a strange feeling that a power over which I had no control compelled me to do it. I seemed to be conscious that something was by my side which would terrify me to look upon, and yet I was impelled beyond all ability to resist to look upon it. I turned my eyes, and they lighted on Paul Sachs, or Peter Graat, as you now call him."

Albert started, and cried, "Dare he enter the cabin without being summoned?"

"He did," replied his wife; "I never heard him approach, and when I saw him a scream arose to my lips, but I stifled it. He remained silent for a minute, and I at length summoned courage enough to inquire what he wanted. He replied, 'A few minutes' conversation with you.' 'A few minutes' conversation,' I reiterated. He replied in the affirmative, and striving to conquer my dread, I assented with a bend of the head, and motioned him to a seat. Of this he took no notice, but speaking in that hollow voice of his he commenced—

"It is useless for me," he said, "to affect an ignorance that you are aware of my acquaintance with the *real* purport of your husband's voyage; or, that in a degree, my destiny is interwoven with his. It would likewise be a folly to pretend that I am not cognisant of your full knowledge of the strange circumstances connected with your husband's family, as far as he has been acquainted with them ; but, you may not perhaps know that I was chief mate on board the Amstelredamme, commanded by Captain Philip Vanderdecken, the father of your husband. He was of a noble, generous spirit, but the victim of a hasty, ungovernable temper. You are aware that he was anxious to return to his wife ; you are aware that for eighteen weeks we beat about the Cape until every man on board was worn to a skeleton, not excepting Captain Vanderdecken, who himself looked a living impersonation of death. The contrary winds and the sickness which baffled efforts produced ; the fatigue, exhaustion, and the excessive excitement which his impetuous temper and adverse circumstances occasioned, I believe, turned his brain, for he acted like a madman. I loved him, madam, as though he was my dearest brother. I knew, likewise, what had produced this painful aberration of intellect; and I believed the wisest plan to save all our lives, and restore him safely to his wife, was to put into Table Bay, and wait for a favourable wind. I spoke to the men, I appealed to him, urged, prayed to him, to accede to my request. He laughed in scorn, he spurned me from him; but still I felt kindly towards him, and with the belief that he would thank me afterwards, I begged the men to assist me in putting him in his cabin, and run the vessel into Table Bay; and this was to save him, his men, and his cargo, as I hope for mercy hereafter. They consented, and advanced to put it into execution. I went first up to him, he struck me with tremendous force ; the ship yawed in the wind at the moment, and I found myself in the raging water. Suddenly I felt as though a hand of fire was placed upon my breast, withering and scorching every drop of blood in my veins ; and a voice thundered in my ears, ' you shall say to him, *Philip Vanderdecken, you are doomed to beat about until the day of judgment.*' The next instant I found myself standing among the crew ; pointing to him I repeated the words, and then my senses were taken from me. While in my trance, a something appeared to me—a shapeless mass, an indescribable thing without a form—a mist, a veil, a mystery, which made it far more horrible than though the most terrific figure had stood before me. A voice issued from it, and said,

' you are chosen as an instrument to work out the decrees of an inscrutible Providence; you are to sail as one of the crew in different vessels, whose destination shall make them pass the Cape ; you will invariably meet Vanderdecken's ship bearing out his doom ; disasters will ensue, and all the souls lost in the event will be added to the amount of sins already against Vanderdecken. You will be permitted to forewarn the Captain of any vessel you may be in of approaching danger after you have met with Vanderdecken ; but, lest the weakness of human nature should make you fail in the duty imposed upon you, I thus impress the attributes of another nature upon you. A hand was stretched forth from the mysterious object, and I felt as though my brow was circled with a coronet of fire, burning, eating into my brain. My blood boiled, danced up and down through my veins, tingling, and pricking me with a strange propensity for malicious mischief. I ground my teeth, and felt, with a kind of devilish delight, a malignity of feeling which cannot be described. The burning brand left my brow, but the fiendish feeling remained. I awoke; I found myself upon a high beach beneath a steep rock. It was a bright sunny morning; I mounted the rock, and a vessel appeared in the offing ; I waved my jacket, they saw me; a boat was lowered, and I went on board. I told them I had been wrecked. We had a prosperous voyage, and I arrived safely in Amsterdam. I changed my name from Peter Graat to Paul Sachs. I soon got a ship, we sailed, and met with Vanderdecken's ship beating against the wind. I pointed it out as a Phantom Ship, and christened it ' THE FLYING DUTCHMAN,' for it appeared in a heavy gale with every sail set, which Vanderdecken, in one of his mad freaks, had compelled the men to do. She disappeared; I cautioned the Captain of danger, and soon after our vessel went to pieces on breakers. In the history of that voyage you may learn that of all I have been engaged in ; but the one I am engaged in now I have a strange presentiment is to be the last. The malignant, fiendish feeling which possessed me, has passed away. Your husband—whom I have looked upon with a horrid desire to tear him piecemeal—is now in my heart as his father was—the first object of my affection. With this I feel a depression. I know that if this is to be my last voyage, I shall meet with death—I hope for it— but I fear that Albert Vanderdecken will also pass away, if he succeeds in averting his father's doom. If such is the case you will be left a wretched widow—for you will be spared, of that I am assured—to pine and waste your life away as Albert's mother did. There is one way to avert this. To save you the agony of such an occurrence, you must obtain from your husband the relic, that piece of the Holy Cross which he wears, and give it to me. The presentation of that cross by his son, for Philip Vanderdecken to kiss upon the deck of his own ship, on the spot where his oath was uttered, are the means, and the only ones by which the doom of Vanderdecken is to be alleviated. If Albert persists in attempting this—although I do not surely know—the result will be he will perish in accomplishing it. If I have the Cross, he cannot succeed : his life will be spared to you, and, although I may still keep as his doomster until the day of judgment, I shall not repine at it ; having spared you a life of misery and anguish.

Albert presents the Cross to his Father.

" I could not answer him," continued Aylmine, "and saying that he would see me again, he quitted the room. What is your opinion of all this, Albert ?"

" I doubt the kindliness of the motive," replied Albert, thoughtfully, " which induced him to persuade you to obtain the cross. I remember, when sailing with him during my first voyage, while anchored off Table Bay, that he attempted one day, while I was asleep upon deck, to steal it from my bosom."

" That was the only time, during nineteen years, that I had a feeling of human kindness pass through my breast. It was to spare you, perhaps, a long life of incertitude and delusive hopes, and your wife one of bitterness and despair ;" cried a hollow voice at his elbow.

Albert started as though he had been stabbed, and turning round, beheld Peter Graat. Aylmine uttered a faint scream, and buried her face in her hands.

Albert recovered himself in an instant, and said haughtily—

" What is the meaning of your intruding into my cabin without being summoned ?"

Peter Graat gave a melancholy smile and waved his hand.

No. 12   N

"Albert Vanderdecken," he said, "the connexion of our destinies must set all ceremony between you and me aside. You know who I am; my history you have learned from your wife. You, therefore, will not look upon me as one of the common herd of mortals, and to be treated as such. But, to the point. You wrong me in believing that I have any other than a kind motive in desiring you to part with the relic. It is for your future comfort I wish—for no end or purpose of my own; but act as you think best. I do not know the end of the mystery that encircles us; but the same presentiment, which tells me on the accomplishment of your undertaking I shall rest in peace, also tells me that your life will pass away. Every ill feeling I had towards you has fled; I speak openly and sincerely. You will now, therefore, exercise your own discretion; either proceed with your task, or, delivering me the portion of the Holy Cross, return to your home and probably die at a happy old age."

"You tell me the end of this mystery is hidden from you, as well as from me?" said Albert, interrogatively.

"I do," was the pilot's reply.

"Then my mind is made up to the course I shall pursue," said Albert, decisively.

"And you will——" suggested Peter Graat.

"Keep my Oath, which is registered in heaven," returned he firmly.

"It is enough!" replied Peter Graat, and quitted the cabin; while Aylmine, throwing herself on Albert's breast, burst into a passion of tears.

CHAPTER XIII.

ALBERT MEETS WITH HIS FATHER.

"Do you think, Aylmine," said Albert, earnestly, "that if it is the intention of the Almighty to take my life if I restore my father to grace, he will spare it, if out of a selfish feeling I refuse to keep a sacred oath under the idea that my life may be spared a few fleeting years? and that only upon a speculation; for did not Peter Graat himself acknowledge the result was hidden from him?"

"He did! he did!" cried Aylmine, "and I know you are right in acting as you intend; but, loving you fondly and dearly as I do, I cannot hinder my affection, displacing justice, and wish you to do almost anything which may afford a prospect of your being spared to me."

Albert was about to reply, when a hurried knock was heard at the door, and upon the entrée being given, the boatswain appeared—cap in hand—saying that a sudden and dense fog had come on, and that Albert's presence was required upon deck. The man quitted the cabin, and Albert, imprinting a kiss upon the brow of Aylmine, followed him.

When he reached the deck, he found it was indeed as the boatswain had stated, for the ship was enveloped in a fog so dense that it was impossible to distinguish from one end of the vessel objects which were at the other. Albert inquired how and when it had approached, and was answered, that it came so suddenly and so rapidly that they were in the thickest of the fog ere they had even notice that there was a haze. As he was not a very long distance from the place where the Johannes had nearly got upon the breakers, he felt anxious respecting the progress the vessel was making through the water, and whether the heavy current, which he knew existed in or near this port, had got the vessel in its power and was sweeping it to shore, or whether his offing was good enough to remove all apprehensions. Navigation was so little advanced at that period that the charts were mostly very imperfect; and the cross-staff being the only instrument by which they could find their latitude and longitude, it is a matter of wonder how, with such blind navigation, they succeeded in making so many successful voyages to long distances. Albert knew the incorrectness of the bearings laid down in the chart, principally from having been the same voyage before, and likewise from the lips of the Captain of the Johannes; who had found Albert so docile and attentive a pupil that he felt a pleasure in communicating all his sea-knowledge to him. Albert had experienced in his present voyage the advantage of his attention to the instruction which the Captain had given him; and now more than ever felt the necessity of drawing upon it to free himself from his present difficulty. The lead was cast, it gave twenty-five fathoms every heave, therefore they had plenty of sea-room, and they could hear no sound of land or breakers; in fact, there was a dead silence. There was no wind, but the vessel was moving through the water they could tell by the ripple at her cutwater. The fog grew every minute more dense, until it reached a darkness greater than the darkest night. It was impossible to see any object at a yard distant, and the men began to get alarmed; Albert also grew uneasy, for with the darkness, the walk of the ship was considerably increased, and there was apparently not a breath of wind stirring. The vessel seemed rushing into some awful gulf without a possibility of arresting its progress. They knew not where they were or where they were going. An hour of this suspense was endured, and the fog began to clear away, almost as rapidly as it had come on. Albert was in hopes that they had only been sailing through a fog bank, and that a few minutes would bring them to a clear sky; but this hope was not realised, for a thick haze still continued; but it was clear enough to see two or three hundred yards beyond the head of the vessel; and it was with much surprise that Albert learned, from one of the men, that a vessel was a-head of them, sailing in the same direction as themselves. He went forward to the bits, and looked with his glass at the vessel, to see if he could make her out at all. She appeared to be of the same build and tonnage as his own; she had every stitch of spare canvas set, and appeared to make about the same progress as the Amsterdammer. Albert watched her with much interest; there was something as strange in her sudden appearance as there had been in that of the fog. She was not a very long distance from his vessel, and he ordered a gun to be got ready forward.

" All ready with the gun, Sir," exclaimed the gunner.

"Fire away," replied Albert.

The gun was fired, but the strange vessel took no notice of it. Albert seized a speaking trumpet and hailed her, but received no answer. There did not appear to be a soul on board her. He determined to come up with her if possible; he ordered, therefore, the reefs to be shaken out of the topsails, and the topgallant-sails set, whereby the speed was accelerated; but, strange to say, did not lessen the distance between the Amsterdammer and the stranger. Albert added sail after sail, until his ship was a cloud of canvas, and flew with extraordinary speed; still, as the rate was increased so did the chase seem to move with additional swiftness through the water, preserving the same distance. Albert followed in her wake, but, to his considerable annoyance, after three hours' chase he did not gain an inch upon the stranger. As his prospect of overtaking her decreased, his anxiety to do so increased. Who or what could she be that thus silently and swiftly ploughed her way through the deep, without one of her crew visible; without anything that betokened life on board; if the spread-sails, done in a style to give credit to the best seamanship, be excepted. On it went without deviating to the right or left; no flag of any description flying; giving birth to no sound; displaying neither bustle or animation, which a ship under a press of canvas always exhibits; and looking like a spectre ship sailing with doomed souls to Pandemonium. Albert started as this idea crossed his mind, and also as he received a slight tap on the shoulder. He turned round and beheld Peter Graat standing at his side; he was surprised to witness the extraordinary change which this man's countenance had undergone. It was still as white as ashes, but the expression was totally different. In place of the fiendish, malicious grin on the features, and the cold, icy glare of the eyes, his countenance had assumed the placid quietness and sweetness which the face of a being presents who in the hour of death, feels happy and calmly resigned to their fate, one who, in the coming change, fondly anticipates the blissful joys of the world to come. Thus looked Peter Graat, and Albert was himself surprised to feel, instead of the shudder which he had always experienced in coming in contact with him, a sympathy, and a yearning of fraternal friendliness spring up in his bosom towards him; and, in the impulse of the moment, he held out his hand and grasped Peter's warmly. The pilot smiled faintly and sadly as he returned the pressure.

"Do you not know the vessel you are taking all these pains to come up with?" he asked.

"No," returned Albert. "I was about to ask you the question, I have watched her these three hours; I have followed in her wake, and set every rag of canvas I could hoist in hopes of overtaking her, without success. I feel an extraordinary desire, indeed quite a gnawing anxiety, to know who and what she is."

"You cannot surmise, then? Look at her name!" said the pilot.

"I have endeavoured to read it, but in vain," said Albert.

"Lend me your glass," said Peter Graat.

Albert did as he requested, and the pilot put the glass to his eye, and after looking a few minutes, he returned it to Albert with a smile, and said—

"Now, Captain Vanderdecken, look, and see how fully your curiosity will be satisfied."

Albert took the glass, and turned it in the direction of the vessel. What was his surprise and amazement on discovering on the stern of the ship, in letters of lambent flame, the words,

Amstelredamme,
Philip Vanderdecken, Master.
1620.

He gazed on it till every drop of blood seemed to forsake his veins. He grew faint and sick, his head grew dizzy; the glass fell from his hand ; he staggered back, and would have fallen, if Peter Graat had not have caught and supported him. In a moment he recovered himself, and turned his eyes in the direction of *his father's* ship, but it was GONE ; not a portion of it was visible. The haze cleared off immediately afterwards, and they found themselves in a clear, bright atmosphere, and close to the spot where the Johannes had gone to pieces. Part of her hull was still visible, and Albert perceived they were standing with every available sail, dead on shore. There was not time for reflection or speculations; the hands—every one that could be of the slightest assistance—were turned up to reduce the sails. This was successfully accomplished in a less time than Albert could have expected, and the ship was put about, but not before they were so close in shore that the lead gave but two fathoms. There was a light breeze up, and the Amsterdammer answered her helm very well. The pilot's knowledge of the coast was of great assistance; and by his steering, and the vessel's performing well, they got once more a very good offing.

"We have escaped that danger, thanks to your excellent piloting," said Albert.

"True," replied Peter Graat; "*that* danger is escaped, but we have a greater to come."

"How ?" asked Albert, surprisedly.

"I know not in what shape it is to come, but I know that it will come ; for I feel upon my spirit the same forewarning that I have ever felt, when some terrible disaster was about to befal a vessel that I have sailed in—after it had met with the 'Flying Dutchman,'" replied the pilot.

"If you know not in what shape it is to come, how shall I prepare for it ?" asked Albert. "It is difficult to provide against a danger when you know not when, where, or how it may attack you ?"

"There is but one way to provide against disasters at sea, which is to see that your boats are in good order to enable you to quit your ship, should any fatal or dire necessity require it," exclaimed the pilot. "This I would have you do ; get stores, spars, masts, sails, and everything ready to be applicable at a moment's notice. That there is a necessity for it I too well know ; that it can not be productive of any harm if, fortunately, not required, you are all well assured."

"It shall be as you say," returned Albert. "Circumstances have told me that you speak not unadvisedly ; and from the change that has come over you, which I have noticed with a gratification which no words can express, gives me every reason to believe that you counsel me for the best. The safety of my people, and of her who is nearest and dearest to my heart—my beloved wife—fill me with a desire to adopt any measures that may counteract the evils which the sight of the fatal Phantom Ship ever prognosticates. The only means I can put into action are those you speak of; we have yet a few hours' daylight, and they shall be used. That accomplished, I shall, until I meet with the danger, pursue the object with which I commenced my voyage."

Peter Graat bowed his head, and walked quietly forward, while Albert gave immediate directions to make the boats ready for immediate use. He called the men aft, and told them that the vessel they had seen and had followed, was the 'Flying Dutchman,' and that it invariably prognosticated the destruction of the vessel to which it made itself visible. "They knew the legend," he said, "and it might be true or not; still," he continued, "we have every right to be careful of our own lives, and of those who depend upon us. Therefore, by being ready to meet a danger we shall, when it comes, rob it of half its distress." The men huzzaed, and went to work with right goodwill. In a few hours, just as daylight was departing, they completed everything necessary to make the boats comfortable and serviceable for a long voyage; and they retired to their hammocks with a foreboding that their rest would be broken by some untoward event. Albert, when he had seen everything completed as he could wish, returned to his cabin, where he found Aylmine waiting anxiously for him.

After an explanation of what had taken place and what was likely to take place, he retired to his cot to sleep. He had been asleep about four hours, a sound, calm, refreshing sleep, when he was awakened by Aylmine, who said the cabin was full of smoke. He started up and found it was as Aylmine had stated; he hastily dressed himself, and running upon deck, gave the alarm to the watch. The sleeping seamen were speedily aroused from their hammocks, and upon deck. Albert directed a party to discover what part of the vessel was on fire, while another party drew buckets of water to quench it. The men sent to discover it, returned hastily, and stated that the lower hold was on fire. It was filled with casks of spirits, and was burning furiously; the smoke, which rolled in dense masses from the hatchway, fearfully seconded the seamen's story; and parties were sent down in gangs with buckets of water; but the fire had taken too fierce a hold of the surrounding objects to be got under, and it drove the men back as they bravely endeavoured to remove those casks from the midst of the flames, to which the fire had not yet communicated. After desperate exertions, Albert found it impossible to get the fire under; and, as he knew there were several barrels of gunpowder on board, there was no time to be lost; the boats were, therefore, tossed out, and everything handed in that could be obtained. Aylmine was put into the long-boat, and Albert saw every man safely out of the vessel, ere he quitted it. His was the last human foot that trod upon the ill-fated vessel. When every one, and everything were as right as circumstances would allow, they pulled away from the burning Amsterdammer. It was still dark though a beautiful night; there was no moon, but myriads of brilliant stars struggled successfully against the darkness, which the absence of the moon would otherwise have produced. When they had reached about half-a-mile from the ship, they paused to see the ravages the fire had made; it had caught the upper-deck, and the wind was blowing it to the fore-part of the ship ; it ran up the rigging swiftly and fiercely, and the shrouds and stays being speedily burned through, the mast, top-mast, and topgallant-mast all fell with terrific violence over the ship's side. While they were gazing at this fearful sight, the whole hemisphere seemed suddenly illuminated; the sky, in the direction of the burning vessel, was glittering with a thousand fiery brands ; a report, like a tremendous crash of thunder, burst upon their ears, and then nearly total darkness ensued. The fire had communicated with the gunpowder-casks, and the Amsterdammer had blow up.

A dead silence ensued, and for several hours it remained unbroken, save by the splash made by the oars in the water, urging the boats forward. The morning came, and the provision was shared and distri-buted, and it was done sparingly, in order to make it eke out longer, should any unfortunate occasion require it. A week passed away and nothing but sky and water was visible; as yet, the men had borne it cheerfully, but when a second week had elapsed, and no sign of aught living but themselves, in that dreary latitude, met their gaze, their spirits began to desert them. The provisions were now decreasing fast, and the allowance, orginally small, was compelled to be curtailed still more. A third week past, and half that crew, which a month preceding were alive, strong, and healthy, were dead. Day after day passed without any sign of a ship, or anything which could betoken relief to them. Life after life was taken from that skeleton crew, until at length, out of all those who had quitted the vessel, *three* only were left ; and those were Aylmine, Albert, and Peter Graat. As the breath quitted the body of the last expiring seaman, Peter Graat, with a melancholy smile, said—

" The hour approaches. Behold!"

Albert turned his faint eyes in the direction in which Peter Graat pointed, and beheld in the horizon a vessel ; as yet it was but a speck, but soon after the mast and spars were visible, the hull rose up on the water, and the tears gushed into his eyes, as he saw the vessel was ap-proaching the boat he was in, which was riding idly in the long-swell of the calm sea. He turned to Aylmine, and pointed out to her the speedy prospect of relief. She pressed his hands, and said, if he was saved 'twas all she asked of Heaven.

In the long period of wretchedness and privation which they had just passed Aylmine had borne up wonderfully well. It was impossible, under such circumstances, for more devoted, constant attention, to have been shown her, than Albert exhibited ; and, to render his anxiety on her account less gnawing, less powerful, she, in the most desolate hour, had striven to appear cheerful and resigned. This exertion of her spirits had probably kept her alive, and the little sustenance which the delicacy of her constitution required, made her at least not suffer, as the others had so fearfully done, for want of food.

A few hours passed away, and the boat was alongside the vessel which

so short a time since had been a speck upon the ocean. Peter Graat
ran nimbly up the side, followed by Albert, while Aylmine, acting
under the advice of Peter Graat, remained in the boat. When Albert
reached the deck, he gazed with horrified astonishment upon the crew;
it seemed as though they were his own crew reanimated, yet still bearing the emaciated, skeleton appearance which they had when dying
from starvation in the boats. He followed Peter Graat, who had been
received with a shout by the men to the poop ; and, then for the first
time it flashed upon his mind that he was standing upon the deck of the
'Flying Dutchman.' The Captain of the Phantom Ship was there, and
advanced to meet him. He looked in his face ; the features were those
of the portrait, of his own ; his heart beat as if it would bound from his
body ; he unclasped the relic from his neck, he held it up in his
hands; panting, and nearly screaming, he cried "My Father !"

"Albert, my dear Son, my honoured, noble boy!" returned Vanderdecken ; "thou hast done thy duty, proudly and nobly. Place the
sacred relic round my neck, and thy task is completed."

Albert rose as his father knelt down, and placed it on his neck. The
tears rolled down the elder Vanderdecken's pallid cheek, as he humbly
bowed himself before the relic, contritely and penitently, and pressing
it to his lips, he crossed himself devoutly. At this moment a strain of
heavenly music was heard, so soft, so exquisitely beautiful, that it ra-
vished Albert's sense, and all recollection of worldly things seemed
taken from him by that sweet sound ; but his father's gentle voice broke
on his ear, and aroused him.

"Albert, my dear Son," said Philip Vanderdecken, "the fearful consequence of my oath has passed away ; my doom is averted, and my
spirit will find repose ; through thy filial love has this been accomplished. Dangers, privations, wretchedness, despair, and anguish, hast
thou borne unrepiningly through my impiety, and for this shalt thou
meet with happiness here, and in the world to come. Should any circumstance arise to give birth to thine anger, remember the consequence
of thy father's rashness, and let thy wrath turn aside. Farewell, Albert ! we shall meet no more in this world. God bless thee ! my beloved, honoured son ; in thy prayers remember the soul of thy father
Philip Vanderdecken."

*   *   *   *   *   *   *   *   *   *   *   *

Years rolled away. A youth, one evening in the suburbs of Amsterdam, endeavoured to accomplish an almost impossible feat. He was a
proud, impetuous youth, and, in his excitement, he was about to utter
an oath that he would succeed in spite of everything ; when his father,
a noble-looking man, who happened to be near, checked him ; and prevented him fulfilling his rash intention. That evening, round a cheerful fire, were seated the father and mother, and four young people ; it
was Albert and Aylmine, with two sons and two daughters. They had
enjoyed, since the accomplishment of Albert's task, an uninterrupted
course of worldly happiness. To his son did Albert relate the effects of
his father's rash oath; and bade him, when a hasty vow rose to his lips,
remember the fate of the FLYING DUTCHMAN !

FINIS.